ANTHOLOGY OF
TERROR

PALMETTO
P U B L I S H I N G
Charleston, SC
www.PalmettoPublishing.com

Paperback ISBN: 9798822955578

ANTHOLOGY OF
TERROR

Ominous Tales of Murder, Mystery, & Mayhem

J. ANTHONY

I dedicate this work to my children, LRK and FJK.
Remember, sheep get slaughtered.
Wolves run free.
Don't be afraid to lead the pack.

CONTENTS

ARE YOU FULL?

When that familiar winter chill first hits the air, I begin to dread each approaching day. The same joyous holiday season so many people cherish brings me nothing but anxiety. It's not because of some repressed childhood memories. Nor for the selfish reason of not wanting to be alone. Nor even for the sheer fact Christmas has morphed into a globally commercialized commodity, its true meaning diminished by corporate retailers. The sole reason I loathe this time of year is a grossly obese megalomaniac named Charles Angus. You see, for the past eight years, I've toiled and grown listless in the packaging department of Mr. Angus's company, Edge Culinary Supply.

My career started off promising enough. Young and eager, I joined the sales department twelve years ago. I actually enjoyed traveling and meeting different vendors and restaurateurs who purchased Mr. Angus's knives and other commercial kitchen utensils. I made a lot of good contacts during this time and was quite successful. I built a large clientele that helped solidify my position within the organization. Angus knew he needed charming hustlers like me to grow his business. You couldn't have put his fat ass in front of people to make a sales pitch. He barely fit into a suit. His breath smelled like a buffalo's ass. And he sweat like a whore in church. Who in the holy hell would buy anything from him?

Anyway, like I was saying, Angus sure didn't hesitate to let me know how important I was to the organization.

"I can't thank you enough, Phil. Closing that deal with the guys from that hibachi chain, Nokuru, is going to earn our company a robust profit. We were really in trouble there for a while. I didn't know if we were even going to make payroll this month. But that order of knives and cleavers will position us comfortably into the upcoming year. And rest assured there's going to be a handsome bonus in it for you, Phil. You've earned it. We wouldn't be in business without you. You're the best at what you do. Keep up the good work."

Those words were so true. I *had* earned it. And I *was* the best. However, as is often the case in life, eventually every wave hits the beach. And when my wave hit, it sure crashed hard.

In the beginning, Angus was tolerable as a boss. He played his role. And I played mine. His attitude started to change for the worse as his company began to expand and grow. The change was subtle at first. But eventually he became a real asshole. Most of this new growth came his way thanks to the advent of the internet and online commerce. Angus was shrewd and savvy enough to pay some tech kid still in college to develop a website for him. As soon as the damn thing went live, the orders started pouring in. Each morning when we opened for business, a list of orders would be waiting to be filled. All this overnight success meant two things: first, Angus became obsessed with power and control, and second, my days as a top producing sales agent were virtually over.

I struggled to keep what few clients I still had. But it was useless. Slowly but surely, every last one of them walked away from me and began to do business strictly online. I really couldn't blame them either. Why waste your time and money going out to dinner and ball games with a sales guy when you could just click a button and get all your materials shipped out overnight? No, I didn't blame them at all.

What really burned my ass was the way Angus gloated and taunted me, like a cat playing with its captured prey before putting the poor creature out of its misery. I still remember the day that fat bastard waddled over to my desk and gave me his ultimatum.

"Well, well, well. Hello, Phil. I have to say your sales numbers are absolutely awful. I should really just get rid of you. You're dead weight around here. You used to be my leading man. What happened to you? Oh wait a minute. That's right. I remember now. I discovered a way to increase my sales without having to pay your bloated commission checks. Now I don't have to throw my money at young hot shots like you anymore. But don't you worry. I'm not going to fire you, Phil. We've known each other way too long for that. Just to show you my heart is in the right place, I'm going to keep you on, buddy. After all, with all the products I'm sending out, someone has to pack the orders for shipment. You do think you can handle that, right, Phil? If not, there's the door. And good luck trying to get another sales job. No company is going to hire someone with numbers as dismal as yours. You're in a tight spot, Phil, with that big mortgage payment, alimony, and child support. What a shame. So what's it going to be?"

I swear I could have killed that fat tub of shit right then and there. I wanted to wrap my hands around his gelatinous neck and squeeze until his eyeballs popped out of his skull. But I couldn't. He was right. I had no other options. I had to take his offer. He had me by the balls. So that following Monday, I started packing his boxes. Knife after knife. Cleaver after cleaver. Carving fork after carving fork. The orders never stopped. Just as I'd get done with one huge shipment, an even bigger one would be waiting. That's how it remained for me. Ten hours a day, six days a week, for the past eight fucking years!

I'm not the only one who has to deal with Angus's shit. Not a single one of us in the company respects the man. He's disrespected and degraded all of us, on multiple occasions. But as bad as the men have it, female employees have it even worse.

Jennie Ortiz reports directly to Angus as his personal secretary. She's had to deal with one hardship after another in her life. After marrying her high school sweetheart, Roberto, she quickly gave birth to two children, Roberto Jr. and Lucinda, who were only a year apart. Roberto Sr. actively served in the military and was a proud and well-respected family man. After his deployment to Afghanistan in 2004, Jennie had done her best to make ends meet. She started working at *Edge* on a temporary assignment for the holiday season and had been with us for only two weeks when she received a knock on her door late one night. It was a major from the US Army along with their priest, Father Guillermo. Roberto Sr. had been killed when the half-track he was riding in struck an IED and exploded.

Jennie had tried her best to keep her family together after the tragedy. She put her faith in God and kept relying on her strong Christian values. Although she stayed positive for her children, the pressures had proved too much for little Roberto Jr. He started hanging around the wrong crowd. By the age of fourteen, he had already been arrested on three separate occasions. He'd been using drugs and was constantly getting into fights. His reckless behavior had earned him suspensions from school numerous times. One of his older friends had given him a fake gun and dared him to hold up the clerk at a local bodega in order to score some quick cash. Always willing to show off his bravado, Roberto Jr. jumped at the opportunity. As fate would have it, the man behind the counter had a gun of his own and shot Roberto Jr. one time in the chest, killing him instantly.

After the funeral, Jennie had all but abandoned her faith. She lost all her optimism and youthful energy. Understandably, she aged dramatically and had fallen into a state of depression. The only reason she got out of bed in the morning and continued to live was for the sake of her daughter Lucinda. That little girl needed her mommy now more than ever. So Jennie did what she had to do to survive and provide for the only family she had left.

Angus knew Jennie was desperate, and he was more than happy to take advantage of her. He would demean her every chance he got, giving her the most sickening and degrading chores. From cleaning the filth out of his private bathroom to taking his sweat-stained clothes to the cleaners, Jennie did it all. One time, the sadist even had the gall to make her rub ointment on a festering, pus-filled boil he had growing on his hairy, ox-like shoulder blade. How that poor girl hadn't vomited afterward is beyond me. Yeah, Angus was a real *class act* through and through.

At the end of each year, Angus takes a group of us out for a holiday dinner. What happens next is torturous. Instead of showing us his appreciation for another successful year, Angus plants his fat ass at the head of the table and begins to preach to us lowly minions how great and all powerful he is. In between crocodile-sized gulps of food, he brings up our short comings and revels in the fact he has so much control over us. Zombie-like, we all just sit there and watch the clock until the night comes to an end.

This year, that behemoth decides to take us to one of those all-you-can-eat Brazilian *rodizio* places, the kind where the servers walk around with huge hunks of meat they carve right in front of you. Each diner is given a card with a green side and a red side. If the green side is facing up, it means you want to continue eating. If the red side is facing up, it means you've had enough.

We're all sitting at the table, eight of us in total, nine if you count Angus twice. Besides Jennie and me, there are AJ and Michael from accounts payable and Raul, Jorge, and Benny all from maintenance. Not a single one of our group is immune to Angus's torments. AJ and Michael are lovers who live openly in a domestic partnership. They're also strict vegans. As far as I know, neither one of them has ever tasted a piece of meat in his life. As for Raul, Jorge, and Benny, these guys are all solid men. They know their shit when it comes to fixing things. They play a vital role in keeping Angus's assembly line running smoothly in order to crank out the products. Yet Angus shows them little appreciation and even less respect.

I have to say it's pretty damn tight at the table, especially with Angus taking up half the real estate. The place is totally packed with patrons feasting on delicacies of beef, lamb, chicken, and pork. Each table is right on top of the next, which makes it very challenging for the servers to scoot in and out while carrying portable carving stations and all that food. A civilized person would have empathy and patience for the staff struggling to do their jobs under these conditions. Not Angus. He starts cracking on these poor guys right from the get-go.

"Listen up, amigo! I'm paying for this meal tonight, and I want you to keep bringing the food until I tell you to stop. You got that, hombre?"

As I mentioned before, this is an authentic Brazilian restaurant. Accordingly, all of the servers and hostesses are Brazilian. I know they place a lot of pride in their culture. To refer to them with the words "amigo" and "hombre" is typical Angus. He's using Spanish words while most Brazilians speak Portuguese. What an imbecile. I could tell by the expression on their faces. They were livid. However, like any good professionals, they bite their tongues, smile, and continue about their business of tending to the customers. For some reason, Angus is particularly ruthless to this young, smaller fellow who appears to be new to the job. Every chance he gets, he would let him have it. Angus insists on calling him *Chico*, even though his nametag reads "Maurice."

"Hey, Chico, give me some more of that flank steak! Hey, Chico, I need a clean fork. Hey, Chico, why is my wine glass empty? Fill it up!" he demands.

I just shake my head and cringe. But to his credit, Maurice keeps his calm the entire time. His facial expression never changes. It remains stoic.

As the night drags on, it's more of the same. Angus takes turns ridiculing each one of us. For the most part, I'm able to tune him out. However, there are still times when he hits a nerve.

"Hey there, Philly Boy."

I hate when he calls me that.

"I was thinking. We've been so busy lately I think it's time to keep the office open on Sundays. Somebody has to be there to make sure orders get packed and processed. And I can't think of a better man than you to get the job done. Wouldn't you agree? I'm sure you won't mind the extra hours, right, Philly Boy?"

His neck fat shakes violently when he laughs. I can't help but notice his mouth is filled with half-chewed meat. And all sorts of food particles shoot off his tongue when he talks. That tongue is the source of my anguish. I start to fantasize about ripping it out so I don't have to listen to his abuse anymore.

Coming back to reality, I sheepishly mutter, "Sure, Mr. Angus. Whatever you say."

Once again, he has me. He still fucking has me after all these years! What the hell could I do? What choice do I have? I have to work. I need the money. My kids depend on me. My blood begins to boil. Just as I'm ready to snap, Jennie touches my leg. She must have seen the look of sheer rage in my eyes. She motions with her eyes toward her diner card, which is now turned to the red side. Jennie has the right idea. Let's end this nightmare of an evening as soon as possible. When I turn mine to red, the rest of the crew follow suit.

Angus is so consumed with his own self-righteous pontification he doesn't even realize he is the only one at the table who is still gorging himself. Seeing our entire group, with the exception of one obese asshole, has finished their meals, the wait staff naturally slows down the frenetic pace and finally begins to tend to some of the other guests. Realizing this, Angus becomes enraged and lashes out at Maurice.

"Chico! Did I tell you to stop serving me? No, I didn't! Let's go, boy. You better keep slicing that meat. I'm not done. Not by a long shot. And neither is anyone else at this table. You keep carving until *I* say stop. Me! *I'm* in charge. Not them. You see this card? It's green. Not red. Even a greasy wetback like yourself should be able to tell the difference between the two colors."

The muscles underneath Maurice's eye twitch involuntarily. It is now clear Angus has gotten to him too. He just stands there staring, either too proud or too stunned to move.

The silence is deafening, but Angus breaks it in one obnoxious instant.

"Jennie! You barely ate a thing. Have some more. I know you don't get to eat like this when you're home. With your husband and son gone, you and your daughter probably do take out most nights. Am I right?"

As Jennie sits solemnly, Angus, still drunk with fury, continues his tirade.

"What about you ladies?" he says, addressing AJ and Michael. "Don't you think it's about damn time the two of you put some *real* meat in your mouths? I mean, come on already. Based on your choice of alternative lifestyle, you should be used to swallowing large, thick objects."

Listening to him, I literally begin to feel light-headed. I close my eyes for a minute and try to refresh my senses. When I open them, I take notice of Maurice. He is standing next to Angus and still has that blank look on his face. He hasn't moved the entire time. In fact, he appears to be in a trancelike state.

I don't know why, but I keep staring at him. Something tells me not to look away. Angus must have noticed me gazing past him at Maurice, which further infuriates him.

"Why are you just standing there, Chico? Do something, for Chrissake. Move your Mexican ass and carve me more meat. Pretend you're running over the border like the rest of your people do. I bet you'd hustle then."

Maurice stands as still as a statue. He doesn't flinch.

"Do you hear me, boy? I said carve me more meat," Angus rages. "I'm still hungry."

The words pierce my brain like a thousand needles.

"I want more meat!"

It feels like a freight train running through my head. My ears are ringing. Sweat is dripping. I can't get any relief from the pressure.

"I want more meat!"

The ringing becomes so intense I begin to feel nauseated. My stomach rumbles. I can't sit still. Can't get comfortable.

"Pick up that carving fork. Stick it in. And carve me more meat!"

I can't take it anymore. I open my mouth to let out a scream, but not a sound comes out.

Suddenly, total silence. It's surreal.

Like a dutiful servant, Maurice follows Angus's orders, just like the rest of us do. He picks up the carving fork, sticks it in, and begins to carve more meat. Let me reiterate. He picks up the carving fork, holds it high over his head, light glistening off the stainless steel prongs, and drives it down with all his might directly into the left side of Angus's throat, straight through his jugular.

Although his eyes widen dramatically, Angus barely makes a sound. His arms stiffen as he drops his utensils. His hands violently clench. His entire body is now in a paralytic state. He gazes upward and to the left just in time to see Maurice's razor-sharp fillet knife slice effortlessly through the repository of neck fat that hangs generously over his collar.

As spurts of blood pump feverishly out of the gaping wound, Maurice gingerly uses his tongs to remove the hunk of flesh, placing it gently on Angus's plate. His body convulses. His eyes dart wildly back and forth. His lips quiver. He feebly attempts to speak but cannot utter a word.

Not believing my own eyes, I notice Jennie reach onto the table in front of her. In wild amazement, I watch her pick up her diner card and turn it over to the green side. Seeing this, Maurice smiles, and with the precision of a surgeon, he expertly begins to dissect more flesh from Angus's bloated carcass. One by one, everyone begins to turn their cards to the green side. Raul, Jorge, Benny, and even the vegans AJ and Michael eagerly turn cannibalistic and feast greedily on huge hunks of raw flesh from the high and mighty Charles Angus. At the same time, the entire dining room erupts in applause.

As I watch my companions savor their meals, blood and tissue dripping from their jowls, my eyes lock with Maurice's. There he stands, grinning over the now shredded remains of the man who has made my life a living hell over the years. I manage to return a half-smile while my hand fumbles for my diner card. Always a team player, I turn it to green.

I did, however, ask Maurice for a special request.

"Maurice, my good man, if you'd be so kind, please serve me his tongue."

Happy to oblige, Maurice goes back to work and finishes his masterpiece.

In the last moments of his life, while gurgling and violently choking on his own blood, Angus watches me devour the root cause of his verbal torment throughout the years. While savoring my feast, I notice a very familiar logo on the butt plate of Maurice's carving utensils. It's a mark I have grown to know well over the years.

I can't help but wonder whether I made that sale. I *would* ask Mr. Angus. But then again, he seems to be at a loss for words.

THIRD SHIFT

The late model Crown Vic sits idling, nestled between two buildings. A once proud and intimidating fleet vehicle, involved in countless pursuits and proactive police work, it is nothing more than a left-over relic, long past its prime. Although the Police Interceptor badge is still prominently displayed on the trunk, this work horse has been demoted to the rank of campus security vehicle.

The occupants are numb to their surroundings. They've been here before...many times...together. He's reclined in the front seat. His dark blue polyester pants are pulled midway down his thighs. As he gets closer to climax, he opens his eyes and glances down at the young woman's head wedged between the steering wheel and his lap. He grabs a fist full of her platinum blonde hair. As she sucks him off, he forcefully bounces her head up and down until he can take it no longer. He uses both hands to hold her head down as he pumps deep into the back of her throat. She swallows most of his load, but the rest drips out and on to his lap as she comes up for air.

"Jeez, Tam. That's gonna leave a stain. These are my only clean pair of uniform pants."

"Are you seriously complaining right now?" Grabbing a wad of D&D napkins from the visor, she says, "Here, use these to clean yourself up. I gotta get back to the club. If I miss another set, Vinny's gonna flip his shit. Last thing I need right now is to get fired."

"Yeah right. Vinny's not getting rid of you, baby. You're his best worker. Plus, you've been giving him head for free for way too long. He owes you."

"Fuck you."

"Maybe next time."

***

Paul Altmann is a washed-up ex-cop from Rahway, New Jersey. He's forty-eight and has been working third shift as a campus security guard at Kean University for the past fifteen years.

Tamara is a twenty-year-old runaway, hardened beyond her years. She met Paul at Breathless Go-Go, where she's a dancer. He knows her only as Tamara, her stage name.

At first, Tamara assumed Paul was like every other creeper who spends his time in a strip club in the middle of the day, pissing away his meager paycheck on girls half his age. But over time, Tamara realized Paul didn't have a lot in common with the other regulars. He was different. Make no mistake, she recognized he was a broken man with some long-repressed issues. But for some reason, Tamara looked at him as a harmless guy who just got dealt a bad hand in the game of life.

Paul and Tamara had been talking on the regular for about a year. In a dancer's world, talking means giving a guy head or fucking him. A lot of the girls earn extra money this way. It's a common story in this dark world. The pills dull your senses, making the vile acts more tolerable. The cocaine that follows propels you back on stage for another set. And the cash in hand provides the justification needed to continue on this twisted cycle.

As time passed, Paul and Tamara became more comfortable with each other. They began meeting more frequently. Sometimes, they stayed up all night conversing. Other times, they fucked their brains out. Tonight was one of those times. They ended up at the Garden State Motor Lodge, one of the few places Paul could afford. Tamara didn't seem to mind. Like Paul, she also knew what it was like to be on the balls of her ass. After being satisfied, Paul decides to open up more than he ever has in the past. He wants her to understand his plight. Plus, in a selfish way, he needs to get his thoughts out. It's cathartic for him. He's tired of keeping everything bottled up inside. Sitting naked in bed, Tamara lights up a Newport menthol. She passes one to Paul and gives him her undivided attention. He takes a long, slow drag to calm his nerves.

***

The year was 2004. Paul was a police officer. A very successful one. He was young, fit, good-looking. He had married his high school sweetheart. The couple had a daughter. Paul earned countless accolades throughout his career. He was sitting number one on the list for the position of sergeant. It was only a matter of time until he got promoted.

One day while on patrol, everything changed. A ten-year-old boy riding a scooter darted into traffic from behind a parked car. By the time Paul reacted, it was too late. He struck the boy with his cruiser, killing him instantly. To make matters worse, the child was the son of the mayor of Rahway – Paul's employer.

There was no negligence on Paul's behalf. Clearly, this was an unforeseen, tragic accident. However, the mayor didn't see it that way. His grief turned to anger. His anger turned to obsession. His obsession turned vindictive. He could not bring himself to promote the man who caused him and his family so much pain. Paul was bypassed for the position of sergeant. His so-called friends and supporters on the job and within the community immediately turned their backs on him. He became a pariah, completely abandoned.

This was the beginning of Paul's decline. Physically, he let himself go. Drinking heavily, he quickly fell out of shape. His career hit a dead-end. He started calling out sick regularly. When he *was* at work, he was consistently disciplined for repeated violations of department policies and procedures. Over the next two years, he was the target of numerous internal affairs investigations, which ultimately resulted in his termination.

Not surprisingly, Paul's home-life was also a disaster. After years of pleading with him to seek counseling for his depression and substance abuse, his wife grew tired and resentful. She left the house, took their daughter, and filed for divorce.

Alone and desperate, Paul was left to ponder his fate. His family was gone. His unemployment benefits had run-out. He had no source of income. Becoming homeless seemed inevitable. He had to get back on his feet. He needed to get back to work. But how? No police department would hire him in his current state. Luckily for Paul, the position of campus security guard was a little less scrutinized.

***

"That was a little more than fifteen freaking years ago, baby. I can't believe it's been that long. I remember it like it was yesterday. Where the hell did the time go?"

Tamara doesn't answer him. She doesn't utter a single word. She just stares off into space with a blank look on her face.

"Tam, you okay? What's wrong, baby?"

"Nothing's wrong. Nothing at all." Tamara gets off the bed to retrieve her purse and begins to rummage through the bag. With her back to Paul, she continues, "What makes you think anything is wrong?"

Without warning, Tamara spins to face Paul, while letting out a hawk-like shriek. With a pair of scissors in hand, held high over her head, she lunges and pierces the top of his deltoid, slicing deep into the muscle. Had Paul not stumbled backward and tripped over the foot of the bed, the steel blades would have been thrust directly between his eyes.

Tamara pounces on Paul and fights with the fury of a wild savage, slashing, biting, and howling. Dazed and covered in his own blood, Paul relies on instincts he thought long left his broken, middle-aged body. With Tamara straddled on top of him, Paul hooks his legs around her calves. He rocks left, then right, using the momentum to reverse positions. He is now firmly planted on top and becomes the aggressor. He uses this much needed leverage to wrestle the scissors away from Tamara and buries them deep into her chest cavity.

Paul stares into her dying eyes. Her breathing is agonal. She coughs up blood. Yet she manages a smile. Her mind travels back in time to the days of her innocence. She was the product of a broken home. Her parents had divorced when she was only four years-old. She had no real recollection of her father. Her mother re-married in an effort to provide Tamara with much-needed stability. However, instead of acting as a father figure, Tamara's new stepfather altered her life forever. For years, he molested her on a daily basis. In the beginning, she blamed herself. The shame was unbearable. But over time, she came to the realization that she bore no fault. She began to harbor resentment against her mother and wondered how the woman could not see what was happening under her own roof. How could she turn a blind eye to the obvious? When Tamara turned fifteen, she had finally mustered up the courage to leave her childhood and her identity behind once and for all.

It didn't take long for the money she had saved to run out. That's when she walked into Breathless for the first time. Looking older than her actual age, she lied and told the manager she was eighteen...not that he cared. All he wanted was his dick sucked, which he got. And Tamara got her set spot.

The years had aged her. She lost her youth. The pills and other drugs clouded her head. However, this particular night became a moment of clarity. The anger Tamara felt toward her mother was immense. But it paled in comparison to the rage she harbored against the man who walked away from her all those years ago. The man who should have fought for her. The man who should have been there to protect her.

In the beginning, she used to pray for his return so he could rescue her. In the end, her prayers were answered. She was finally free of the inner demons that plagued her over the course of her life.

The adrenaline dump causes Paul's heart to race like it is about to break out of his chest. Searching for an answer, he uses his swollen, chopped up fingers to sift through the contents of Tamara's purse. When he finds what he's looking for, it all becomes clear. The driver's license he holds in his hand explains everything.

With her last breath, Nicole Jessica Altmann utters her final words.

"Thank you, Daddy. I love you."

Although in a state of shock, Paul demonstrates his natural paternal skills and replies, "You're welcome, Nicole. I love you too."

SOUTHERN HOSPITALITY

Stonewall Confederate Cemetery, Winchester, Virginia

Kelly Dougherty and Ian Murtagh are in their mid-twenties and have been together since college. Born into the millennial generation, their sense of entitlement borders on obscene. Like true ideologues, uncompromising in their beliefs, they are mere products of a society that promotes social justice and, at times, outright lawlessness. As such, they've been on a crusade of sorts, in their eyes, to right the injustices of the world. Kelly and Ian have spent the summer jockeying from town to town, protesting and kibitzing with other cohorts of similar values, wreaking havoc and instilling fear upon an already fragile and divided country.

Currently, the two find themselves in the hills of Northern Virginia in the town of Winchester, staring at the gates of the Stonewall Confederate Cemetery. Established in 1866, Stonewall is the resting place of nearly twenty-six hundred Confederate soldiers, who died in the surrounding areas during the war. Some of the most notable inhabitants are Brigadier General Turner Ashby, better known as the "Black Knight" of the Confederacy, and Colonel George Smith Patton, grandfather of the legendary General George S. Patton, commander of the US Army during World War II. The burial plots are segregated by state, making it easier to locate particular individuals. Directly in the center of the park stands a solemn memorial, which is dedicated to the unidentified soldiers who paid the ultimate price during battle. The remains of over eight-hundred men have rested peacefully and undisturbed on this very spot for more than a century and a half. However, two overzealous activists are about to change all that forever.

"We're finally here. Stonewall Confederate Cemetery."

"Yeah, this is it all right."

"This place is wrong on so many levels. As far as I'm concerned, it never should've been built in the first place."

"Maybe so, Kelly. But I'm still not sure about this. Protesting is one thing. But desecrating a national cemetery, even a Confederate one, just doesn't seem right."

"What are you unsure about, Ian? Are you unsure if these racist demons fought for the Confederacy? Or if they owned slaves? Or if they oppressed our black and brown brothers and sisters for hundreds of years?"

"No, it's not that."

"Then what it is?"

"I don't know. I just feel we might be going too far. I mean, the Civil War ended almost a hundred and sixty years ago. What do any of these people have to do with what's happening in the world today?"

"Oh my God. Are you for real? These people are the forefathers of modern-day xenophobes. They epitomize the systemic racism that still plagues America to this very day. There shouldn't be *any* statues or monuments celebrating them. This is another form of white privilege. These animals should be erased from history all together."

"Kelly, listen. I'm all for change. You know that. And I totally agree with you that these men were evil in their time. All I'm saying is we need to be careful. After the looting at the protest last night, we were lucky to get out of D.C. without spending the night in jail."

"Jail? We're not going to jail. In these big cities, the politicians own the police. And our movement owns the politicians. Trust me. No mayor or wannabe governor is going to risk their campaign in defense of a few ultra-conservatives who are stuck living in the past. Don't you see? *We're* the future. Not them. When we're done here, they're going to build monuments for *us*. People like you and me are the ones who are going to be remembered for greatness. We're the true heroes."

"You're right, baby. You're always right. Fuck these white trash hillbillies. Let's do this."

"Yes! Let's go re-write history."

***

As the pair walk along the darkened labyrinth, flanked on either side by live oaks and sycamore trees, they find themselves engulfed in the rich, Southern tranquility. The gentle moonlight illuminates the walking path and guides them to the object of their dismay. Standing nearly fifteen feet in height, the immense obelisk towers over the young lovers. The two-ton slab of concrete is adorned with an ornate carving of a Southern infantry regiment engaged in battle. A mighty bronze statue of the company commander perched atop his horse rests high on the base.

"Well, what do we have here?" asks Ian.

"Looks to me like we found what we're looking for," answers Kelly, as she reads the words inscribed at the base.

To the 800 souls who perished upon this hill, you are not forgotten. You fought valiantly to defend our land against the invaders during the War of Northern Aggression. Let us not weep for you. Instead, let us take solace knowing one day the South Shall Rise Again. Hail Dixie!

"What a bunch of crap. I mean, 'the South Shall Rise Again.' Please. Here's what I think of the South."

A precisely aimed wad of spit flies from Kelly's pursed lips and lands squarely on the epitaph.

With a laugh, Ian applauds her effort, "Nice shot, babe. But I think it's about time we *really* get to work."

"I couldn't agree more."

Ian pulls out a masonry hammer from his duffel bag and taunts the fallen warrior.

"Time for an *upgrade*, General."

With each swing, jagged pieces of stone fly in every direction. A thick cloud of cement dust pollutes the once clean and crisp Southern air. Before long, the mural is unrecognizable. Its glorious imagery lies crumbled at the feet of the vandals.

Like an impatient child anxious to open her Christmas presents, Kelly squeals, "My turn, my turn," and proceeds to decorate what's left of the stone with a generous portion of spray paint. She has honed her graffiti skills over the past several months, and she impresses Ian with her masterpiece.

"Damn, babe. I didn't realize how artistic you are."

"What can I say? This girl's got talent."

"You certainly do. But something is still missing."

"You think?"

"Yeah. It needs a final touch. And I know just the thing."

Ian easily scales the monument, using the portions of chipped away block as a make-shift ladder. Grabbing onto one of the horse's legs, he hoists himself up to the top.

"Toss me my bag, Kel."

"Here you go."

"Got it. Thanks."

Digging into his bag once again, Ian is now armed with a reciprocating saw and goes to work on the aged material. The high-intensity buzzing screams through the night, as metal on metal friction produces a steady stream of sparks until the blade comes to rest.

"We just have to get through two of the legs. Then, with a little luck, its own weight should easily bring it down."

Reliving her days as a high school cheerleader, Kelly enthusiastically supports her man.

"Keep going, baby. You got this."

With the saw once again in full-power mode, Ian resumes the task at hand. Cutting the second leg, however, proves much more laborious than did the first. With aching forearms and beads of sweat dripping from his forehead, Ian powers through his near exhaustion until finally the statue starts to list. The sound of creaking metal and cracking bolts is followed by a thunderous boom, as both man and beast topple to the ground below. A fallen general and his stallion lie twisted in a heap under the starry night, a far cry from the once majestic team who dutifully guarded this most sacred of tombs.

As the couple strolls away from the carnage, they giggle and reminisce about their latest accomplishment, eagerly anticipating the next stop of their movement to rid the country of its stained history.

Caught up in the moment, the two frolic along without a care in the world. They lose track of time and continue their trek until Kelly voices her concern.

"Is it me, or does it seem like it's taking us a lot longer to get out of here than it did coming in?"

"No, it's definitely not you. I guess I wasn't paying much attention. But you're right. We *have* been walking awhile now."

"Did we go the wrong way or something? Because none of this looks familiar to me."

"How should I know? I was following *your* lead, Kel."

"Well, I was just following the path. I assumed it was the same one we came in on."

The dark Southern evening now appears much less inviting than it did several hours earlier at twilight. Cicadas, barred owls, and other creatures of the night provide a musical melody for their unruly guests. However, it is a faint sound lingering in the distance that is much more alarming. The high-pitched barking howl, a phantom of a noise, intensifies as the source draws nearer, causing the hair on the backs of Ian's and Kelly's necks to snap to attention.

As a sharp chill creeps wickedly down his spine, Ian wonders aloud, "What the fuck is that?"

"I don't know," answers Kelly. "And I don't want to find out. Let's just run."

"Run where? We're fucking lost, remember?"

"I don't know, Ian. Anywhere but here."

Although the couple tries to distance themselves, they remain plagued by the reverberating bellow, which continues to grow stronger and stronger. Suddenly, a new sound enters the fray. Paralyzed with fear, the interlopers listen intently to the rhythmic beat of hooves cantering in the dirt. Hooves closing in on them. At full gallop, hot breath blazes out of the muzzle of the beast. It descends upon the doomed couple with a furious and unapologetic vengeance. The rider, who sports the full regalia of a highly decorated Southern general, leads the charge of a wildly incensed cavalry company hell-bent on revenge. Their Confederate war cry, commonly known as a Rebel Yell, is the last sound Ian and Kelly will ever hear.

***

The next morning, as bright rays of sun peek through the thick, summer foliage and shine onto the hallowed grounds, a tour guide leads a group of children from a local summer camp. He educates his followers about the Civil War, focusing on battles that occurred in the immediate area. As it has for the past century and a half, the relic of the unknown soldiers stands erect in all its glory. As a long-time employee of the Southern Historical Society, this particular guide has given hundreds of tours throughout the years and is intimately familiar with each and every monument. However, something is peculiar. He studies the pristine carvings of the soldiers engaged in battle. He glances upward at the horse-mounted leader, whose condition is remarkable, unscathed from the elements after all these years. As the group moves on, he is left bewildered that *something* is just a little bit different. Perhaps it is the glimmering morning sun that causes him to squint, or the chattering of the raucous group of adolescent boys diverting his attention. Whatever the cause of the distraction, the guide's normally well-trained eye overlooks a subtle, yet noticeable, detail. No longer completely stoic, the general is now showing off his new *smile*.

Scattered throughout the park, hidden under newly minted shallow graves, lie the remains of two self-proclaimed social justice warriors. The inevitable decomposition of their wretched corpses will serve as fodder and nurture this fertile field for years and years to come. Ian and Kelly set out to change history. And they did, just not in the way they anticipated. Instead, they have become two more casualties in a war that is far from *civil*.

BRAGGING RIGHTS

Thompson, Pennsylvania has always held a special place in my heart. It's my home-town. In fact, I still live there today. My name is Jimmy Malcolm, and in the 1960's, Thompson was a wonderful place to grow up. A typical suburbia, streets were lined with overgrown oak trees that created a shady oasis on those hot summer days. Elegant Victorian houses proudly stood guard over their neatly manicured lawns. On any given day, you could hear children of all ages playing outside. It was time to come home when the street-lights came on and they heard the sound of their mothers' voices calling their names. At that time, crime was all but nonexistent. Most people kept their doors unlocked and slept with their windows open. Neighbors watched out for one another. It was a different era – a cleaner era, one of innocence and family values – a much simpler time indeed.

The town center consisted mainly of mom-and-pop shops and the municipal building, which housed the police and fire departments. The only other notable landmark in Thompson was the McClure Asylum for the Clinically Insane, which stood atop Roosevelt Hill. Located on the highest point in town, this towering structure overlooked the entire Thompson Square. McClure was a century-old fortress originally built as a prison to house Civil War detainees. After the war ended, it remained operational as a state prison. However, over the years, budget cuts and deterioration caused McClure to shut down. It wasn't until years later that it was resurrected and transformed into its current role: a maximum-security facility for psychopaths and sociopaths alike. They may have escaped their minds, but there is no escaping McClure.

Back in its heyday, Thompson had a lot to offer its residents. There was no shortage of activities for both the young and old. The highlight of every year came in the fall when the crisp autumn air carried the sweet scent of freshly baked apple pie throughout the entire neighborhood. The Thompson Fall Festival was the anchor of this glorious time. Each year, this gala commenced on October 24 and culminated on October 30, Halloween Eve. Besides rides, food, and entertainment, the fair also held a contest that quickly became an obsession for most of the local children.

The basis was quite simple: design the most creatively decorated haunted attraction. All of the patrons at the festival got to vote for their favorite display. Young boys and their fathers would spend hours on the weekends designing scenery, rudimentary mannequins, and other types of props. Mothers and daughters would sew costumes for the newly developed creations. The rules were clear. All entrants received a space at the fair a week in advance in order to work. These spaces were private and cordoned off to ensure secrecy. No one was able to see finished projects until unveiling them on Halloween Eve. As time passed and the popularity of the festival grew, a competitive nature really began to emerge. Bragging rights were at stake. And let's face it. For an adolescent male, bragging rights for an entire year meant everything.

Lenny Young was three years my senior. He came from a very prominent and affluent family. His grandfather started a coal-mining company at the turn of the century. Lenny's father was in charge of the company. However, it was only a matter of time until Lenny took over the entire lucrative operation. For five straight years, Lenny dominated the competition. He used his cronies – Brett Cox, brothers Rusty and Matt Harper, Roger Carlson, Manny Rivera, and Andrew Corrigan – to help him overcome and demolish any formidable adversary who attempted to take his crown. Breaking into private booths to steal or destroy props was common practice among this group of heathens. They would intimidate and bully other kids into voting for Lenny's designs, even using physical force when necessary. And when all else failed, Lenny would ask his father to use his influence to politic for him in order to get the winning votes. It got so bad that other kids stopped entering the contest. Nobody wanted to deal with Lenny's wrath. He could be relentless. Looking back, it was truly pathetic the lengths these boys went to just to win some silly childhood contest. To this day, it still boggles my mind that none of the adults in town had the courage to step in and stop the nonsense. I suppose this was because a lot of the men in Thompson collected their paychecks from Lenny's dad. Many of them worked at his facility in one capacity or another.

My dad, on the other hand, was different. He was a hard-working man – up every morning at five and off to his place on the assembly line at the Thompson Electrical Components Factory. He tried his hardest to provide for us but always seemed to fall a little short. It wasn't because he didn't have the work ethic. He just couldn't keep away from the bottle of whiskey waiting for him at the end of his shift. He pissed away every dollar he made at the local tavern, Morley McGovern's, leaving us practically penniless.

This vicious cycle continued up until the time I turned thirteen. I remember Dad coming home drunk one night and telling Mother, me, and my brother, Jack, that he was going out west to Colorado to work at some stereo equipment store one of his war buddies had started. He was supposed to be the lead electronics man. He told us everything was going to work out, and he would be able to move the rest of the family out there as soon as he got established. In the meantime, he promised to send back money each week to help Mother with the expenses. I knew at the time these were empty promises, and we would never see Dad again.

Needless to say, his alcoholism had followed him in his westward journey. What's more, the store eventually went out of business, leaving Dad unemployed and ultimately homeless. He ended up begging for money during the day and drinking it away on the streets at night. One night, Mother received a call from authorities informing her they'd found my father dead outside a pool hall in a seedy part of Colorado Springs. All he had in his possession was some loose change, his old work identification card from Thompson Electrical, and a picture of Jack and me as children. Because Mother didn't have the money to have his body shipped back east, Dad was buried in a potter's field, where he remains today. From that point on, it was official. The three of us were on our own.

To say Mother had her hands full trying to raise us would be an understatement. While I was the rebellious one, Jack had his own set of issues because of his condition. He had nearly drowned as a child, leaving him with severe brain damage. Physically, Jack was a fully developed adult male. He was strong as an ox but had the mentality of a six-year-old. He was unable to understand the difference between right and wrong. Jack was never far from Mother's side and seldom left the familiar confines of our childhood home. Mother had to tell him what to do at all times. From my earliest recollections, she never had a free moment to herself. There is little doubt in my mind the constant and relentless attention Jack required contributed to Mother's own health problems.

She slowly deteriorated over the years until the stress and burden eventually caught up to her. It wasn't until years later that the magnitude revealed itself. Mother suffered a stroke and lingered in a semi-catatonic state. The good Lord finally called her home three years later.

The year Dad left, I was determined to create the most realistic Halloween scenery ever, finally beating Lenny Young at his own game. I was the only kid who didn't give a damn about what he could do to me. So it was just the two of us in an adolescent showdown for bragging rights. And like I said before, for a kid in a go-nowhere town like Thompson, a year of bragging rights was worth its weight in gold.

I worked tirelessly both day and night, before and after school. Although it was tough at first, I got the hang of it pretty quickly. The night of judging was only a week away, and things were really coming together nicely. I constructed a giant graveyard, pieced together a few mannequins, and dressed them with some clothes Dad left behind. Then, I put the mannequins in coffins I built out of old pieces of timber from an abandoned barn on Warren Avenue. The whole thing looked pretty realistic in the dark. In fact, I was so confident, I began boasting to my classmates about my inevitable pending victory. But as you can imagine, living in a fishbowl of a town like Thompson, it didn't take long for word to get back to Lenny.

I still remember the day he and his lackeys cornered me in the locker room during gym class.

"Listen, penis breath. You better withdraw from the contest if you know what's good for you," Lenny demanded.

"Not a chance," I shot back, as I laughed in his face.

That's when things really got ugly.

First, Andrew Corrigan sucker punched me. He was always the weasel of the group. Although stunned, I tried my hardest to fight my way out of there, throwing wild punches in every direction. However, my futile attempt at defending myself only fueled their rage. Coming at me from all sides, they quickly overwhelmed me. The Harper brothers held down my arms as Lenny, Brett, and Roger took turns punching and kicking me. Manny stood guard at the door to make sure no teachers were coming. The more I struggled to break free, the more furious the beating.

The whole time, Lenny kept taunting me with insults.

"What's the matter, Jimbo? Your dead drunken dad isn't here to help you. Maybe you should call your mommy. That whore's probably at home wiping your retarded brother's ass."

These words echoed in my ears and burned into my brain. When I could no longer stand on my own two feet, the Harper brothers dropped me directly into a piss-filled urinal. Bloodied and semi-conscious, I remember getting spit on and hearing the sound of sinister laughter.

The last thing I recalled before blacking out was Lenny's voice.

"Now let's go see what this panty waste has been up to."

Eventually, I regained consciousness and dragged myself to the fair-grounds. The lock on my stall had been cut. All of my creations were destroyed. As my anger grew, I became determined to rebuild. I would have to start from scratch with less than a week to finish.

***

On October 30, the day of the contest, Lenny finds a note stuck to his locker at school.

"Jimmy hasn't quit. He's been rebuilding all week. Meet me and the guys at the fair tonight. We'll wreck his work and finish this little ass-wipe once and for all.
-Roger"

Lenny is incensed. He can hardly wait until night-fall to rush down to the fair to teach Jimmy a lesson for the last time. At exactly seven p.m., one hour before the opening of the contestant area to the public, Lenny hops the fence and finds himself face to face with Jimmy.

"Hello, Leonard. How's it going?"

Perhaps it's the tone of Jimmy's voice, or the devilish look in his eyes. It could have even been the fact that he called Lenny by his birth name. No matter. Lenny's instincts tell him something just isn't right.

"I bet you're wondering where everyone is: Brett, Rusty, Matt, Manny, Roger, Andrew. They were supposed to meet you here, weren't they?"

Lenny remains silent as beads of sweat form on his brow. He stands anxiously before his foe as Jimmy continues, "Relax, Lenny. You're not alone. All your friends are here. As a matter of fact, here comes Roger now."

As if on cue, an ominous, hulking figure emerges from the darkness – it is Jimmy's brother, Jack. He holds the severed head of Roger Carlson in his hand and sticks it on top of a stake protruding out of the ground. Jack is also dragging the headless corpse by one of its feet and releases it at the foot of the stake. At this point, Jimmy plugs in an extension cord, which reveals a macabre scene of bloody carnage.

A long steel rod pierces the anus of Brett Cox. It travels deep through his thoracic cavity and exits his mouth. He is hog-tied to a make-shift barbecue rotisserie and is slowly roasting over an open flame. The rancid smell of burnt flesh lingers and permeates the cool evening air. Embers creep higher and higher as the oily meat particles seep off his carcass and drip into the pit of fire.

The Harper brothers are naked, seated back-to-back, and wrapped tightly together with duct tape. Rusty sits disemboweled; his innards hang from his lap and spill to the ground below. Matt's genitals have been severed and are currently protruding from his mouth after being stuffed there. His body is stark white from the voluminous loss of blood.

The claw end of a hammer is buried so deep into the back of Manny Rivera's cranium only the wooden shaft is still visible. Blood gushes from his mouth, nose, and ears.

An old-fashioned Whitehead gag props open Andrew Corrigan's mouth. An empty bottle of hydrochloric acid lies at his feet. Both his top and bottom lips have completely disintegrated. The little flesh that remains is covered in a festering puss that oozes over his facial tendons. His teeth remain anchored into his jaw-bone, forming a skeletal death mask.

For Lenny Young, time stands still. Unable to speak, he is completely paralyzed with fear. The sound of urine trickling down his trembling leg onto the ground below breaks the silence.

Jimmy rages, "You pompous piece of shit! Your own arrogance blinded you so completely that you didn't even realize one by one your friends started to disappear. *All* that concerned you was humiliating me yet again!"

He takes a deep breath and calms himself in order to savor the moment before continuing.

"So what do you think, buddy? Not too bad, huh? I think this year I finally have you beat. You know, Jack and I really worked hard on this. We put in a lot of effort — and in such a short period of time too. You really didn't leave us much choice after you and your crew wrecked my original designs the other day. Truth be told, I should probably thank you. Clearly, this new display is much more realistic than that boring old graveyard. I guess in a weird way, you actually inspired me. At first, I really didn't know how I was going to pull this off. But then I thought of Jack. He's always willing to help me any way he can — does anything I ask. When I told him what had happened and what I needed, he was more than eager to get started."

Suddenly realizing his fate, Lenny sobs uncontrollably and begs for his life.

"Jimmy, I'm sorry. I...I didn't mean any of it. I always liked you. It was the other guys. They made me do it. They hated you. Not me. Please, Jimmy. I don't want to die. I just want to go home."

"Enough! Come on, Lenny. Stop all that whining and blubbering. It's really unbecoming of someone of your stature."

"But please, Jimmy. Pleeeease..."

"Aren't you at least a little impressed? I thought the hard part was going to be luring each one of you parasites into our little trap. It turned out *that* was the easiest part of all. You know that note you found on your locker telling you to meet Roger here? Well, all of you dipshits got the same damn note! Every last one of you thought you were invincible – thought you had carte blanche to do whatever you wanted, without consequences for your actions. Well, Lenny, Jack and I are here to tell you differently. But I guess none of that really matters now."

"No, Jimmy! No!"

"Jeez, look at the time. It's getting late. People are starting to file in already. The voting will start soon. I suppose the only thing left to do is put the finishing touch on our project here and hope for the best. The crowd is really going to love what we did. I can feel it in my bones."

"Oh my God! Please, don't do this, Jimmy! I'm begging you!"

"Yes siree. I can feel it in my bones. Speaking of bones, I think the perfect addition to this masterpiece would be a life-size skeleton. Yes, that's what we need. Do you agree, Lenny? I know Jack does."

"Uh huh. Jack agrees, Jimmy."

"I know you do, Jack. You're such a good boy. Let's show Lenny just how good you are. Show him what you can do. Skin him alive, Jack! Skin the bastard alive!"

33

In an instant, Jack pounces on Lenny with the quickness and ferocity of a lion capturing a gazelle. The mass of Jack's 260-pound frame makes Lenny easy prey. The noises of the carnival drown out the shrieks of agony and cries for help. And thus, Lenny Young is forever immortalized as part of the main attraction at the Thompson Fall Festival. It really is quite an honor. And Jimmy got his bragging rights for a long, long time.

Epilogue

That was so many years ago. Yet I remember it like it was yesterday. Thompson has certainly changed a lot since then. It really is a shame. At least I can still see the fairgrounds from my room though. I wonder if there will ever be another contest. Jack and I would love to defend our title. Being locked up in McClure all these years has given us plenty of time to think of new ideas for an even bigger and better display.

"Isn't that right, Jack?"

"Uh huh. Jack thinks that's right, Jimmy."

"You know, it's almost time for lunch, Jack. I wonder what they're serving today. Maybe fish sticks...or sloppy joes. You really like sloppy joes."

"Uh huh. Jack likes sloppy joes, Jimmy."

"Or maybe it's hot dogs...or chicken fingers. *Those* are your favorite."

"Uh huh. Jack's favorite are chicken fingers, Jimmy."

"You're such a good boy."

THE AWAKENING

Psychiatric Office of Bruce Hirshberg, MD, Livingston, New Jersey

David Kovar sits among the other patients, anxiously awaiting his turn. The events of the past few months have consumed him, his head cluttered with paranoia. He is haggard, partially from lack of sleep, but mostly from the fear of the unknown. He is in desperate need of answers. Answers that have eluded him thus far. As he prays for a rational explanation, the office door swings open.

"Good morning, David. I'm Doctor Hirshberg."

"Hello, Doctor. Thanks for seeing me on such short notice."

"Please come in and have a seat. Make yourself comfortable."

Doctor Hirshberg has been in the practice of psychiatry for nearly thirty years. He is an expert in the field of psycho-analytics.

"I've had time to review your initial screening papers and understand you've been having some troublesome dreams as of late."

"Yeah, that's an understatement."

"Can you elaborate?"

"Well, they're more than just *dreams*, Doc. They're real."

"Real? What do you mean when you say, 'They're real'?"

"I mean *real* shit is happening all around me. And I don't know how to stop it."

"I'm sorry, David, but I'm a bit confused. Are you saying actual events are occurring, or that you've been having vivid dreams that you think are real?"

"Listen, Doc. I don't *think* they're real. They *are* real, damn it! Now, stop twisting my words around and help me figure this out."

David's emotional outburst causes an awkward silence to linger in the air. He takes a moment to compose himself and continues, "I'm sorry. I don't...I don't mean to get shitty with you, Doctor. It's just that I'm so afraid. My stress level is through the roof. I'm barely eating. My sleep pattern sucks. I'm petrified to close my eyes because of what might happen next."

"I understand. It's perfectly normal to let our emotions get the better of us from time to time. Clearly, you have a lot on your mind. Why don't you start from the beginning? That way, I can have a better idea as to how I can best help you."

David sits back in his chair and mentally prepares himself to recount the most disturbing time period of his life. With a long sigh, he clears his throat and begins.

"They started out innocent enough."

"What did?"

"The dreams."

"Okay. Go on."

"The only thing I remember about the first dream is a series of numbers. I had no idea what made those particular numbers come to me in my sleep. All I know is they were crystal clear in my head when I woke up in the morning. When I told my wife, Sharon, about them, she said I should play the lottery. At first I laughed because I never gamble. But then I thought to myself, 'Take a chance.' So I bought a ticket that morning on my way to work. Later that night when I checked the numbers, I realized I had hit five out of six numbers. Obviously, I didn't win as much as I would've had I gotten all six correct. But I still ended up clearing a little over $10,000."

"That's phenomenal, David. Good for you."

"Yeah, tell me about it. Money was tight because we had a lot of credit card debt. It couldn't have come at a better time. We were able to pay off the balances on our cards and even had some left over to put toward our savings."

"That's a great story, David. I'm glad you put the money to good use. But I must tell you there have been hundreds of documented cases in which people have won the lottery after dreaming about numbers. As a matter of fact, it's quite common. I'm assuming there's more?"

"Uh, yeah. There's a lot more."

"Okay. Continue."

"I'd say it was a couple of weeks later when it happened again."

"You're referring to more dreams?"

"Yes. Anyway, I work as a research assistant at a pharmaceutical company. We were working on an experimental drug to treat diabetes. For months, our team had been struggling to figure out the proper chemical composition but couldn't come up with anything solid. The company had already spent millions on R&D but had nothing to show for it. Management had made the decision to scrap the entire project the very next day. That night, I went to sleep restless with my mind racing. Next thing I remember is waking up with a fresh set of ideas, completely different from anything we'd previously tried. You see, the formula had come to me in my sleep, again in the form of a dream."

"So you were able to go forward with the project?"

"Yes. We had a major breakthrough, and I got promoted to vice president of operations. I ended up getting a six-figure bonus also. Sharon and I were finally able to move out of our apartment and into our dream house in the suburbs."

"Congratulations, David. Hard work certainly pays off. But again, I'm not really hearing anything remarkable here. It seems as though these dreams have afforded you some very good fortune."

Perplexed at the blasé analysis, David lashes out.

"Really? What's with the condescending tone?"

"David, I'm just trying to establish a positive correlation between the events you've described and your sub-conscious thoughts. Keep going, please."

"Whatever, man. You made me lose my train of thought. Where the hell was I?"

"You mentioned something about purchasing a new house for yourself and your wife."

"Oh, yeah. Like I was saying, we moved into the house and started working on having a family. For the longest time, Sharon and I tried to have children but were never able to conceive. Eventually, we both went for tests. Turns out she has a rare condition that severely hinders her ability to conceive, let alone carry to term. We had come to the realization that having biological children just wasn't in the cards."

"And is that something you can accept?"

"I suppose. But now it's a moot point."

"How so?"

"Because the first weekend after moving into our new home, a miracle happened. Sharon became pregnant."

"Congratulations."

"Thank you. But what concerns me is the fact that I dreamed of her pregnancy the night of the conception."

"The miracle of life is the most precious miracle of all. You both must be very elated. But I'm still not convinced there is any solid connection between your stories and the dreams you've been having."

Once again, David is taken aback by Doctor Hirshberg's apparent lack of empathy. He sits stoically but cannot hide his displeasure as the doctor continues, "The situations you've described do, however, sound like they fall into the category of precognitive dreams."

"And what is that supposed to mean, Doc?"

"Well, in simple terms, precognitive dreams give us information about our future that we wouldn't otherwise have. What's more, precognitive dreams fall under the broader category of the cognitive theory of dreams. Those who subscribe to this philosophy believe that dreams actually help us organize and interpret our everyday life experiences. The fact is most dreams tend to reflect ordinary events in our daily lives. Basically like the ones you've described to me today."

"I'm sorry, but did you just say *ordinary*?"

"I did."

"*Ordinary*?"

"Yes, ordinary. Is the term *coincidental* more to your liking?"

"That's it. Listen to me, you arrogant prick. See all those fancy diplomas hanging on the wall behind you? Well, you can wipe your ass with them because that's exactly what they're worth. Shit! All the theories and technical jargon you keep spewing is just smoke and mirrors, Doc."

"David, calm down, please. I'm only trying to help."

"You're not trying to help. If you were *really* trying to help, you'd stop patronizing me and start taking me seriously."

"All right. I'm sorry. I'll try to keep more of an open mind. I just want to get to the bottom of what's really troubling you."

"Trust me, you will, because things are about to get dark."

"What do you mean by that?"

"Well, for starters, we put down our dog last month after he was hit by a car right in front of our house. The poor thing was suffering so badly we didn't have a choice but to euthanize him."

"Go on."

"Do you remember the NJ Transit bus crash from two weeks ago?"

"I think so. Didn't the driver have a heart attack behind the wheel?"

"That's the one."

"Yes, unfortunately I do. If my memory serves me correctly, a woman was also killed."

"That's right. The bus jumped the curb and pinned her against a utility pole, crushing her to death right in front of her two kids."

"What an absolute tragedy."

"You're right, Doc. That was a tragedy. But let's not stop here. How about we talk about the building fire in Bridgewater from last week? It was caused by an explosion at a chemical lab. Eight people were incinerated, burned alive."

"What are you getting at, David?"

"Jesus Christ, you're still not putting it together."

"Putting *what* together?"

"I'm the cause of it all!"

"How do you figure?"

"Because I *dreamed* we buried our dog at my parent's summer home in the Poconos. I *dreamed* of a bus crash that killed a lady. And I *dreamed* about people being killed in a fire. And, and…"

"And, what, David?"

"And I'm positive I'm going to be the next to die!"

"What makes you think that?"

"Because the explosion was at *my* lab! All my co-workers are dead. The only reason I wasn't there is I took the morning off to go to an obstetrician appointment with Sharon. I should be dead too!"

"I see."

"Oh, now all of a sudden you see. Well, how convenient considering our hour session is just about up. Let me ask you this. Would you consider these *ordinary* events? But before you answer, I have to tell you one more thing."

"And what's that, David?"

"I thought it over and decided the term *coincidental* is *not* more to my liking."

"All right, David. Here's what I'm going to do. First off, I'm going to write you a script for Prozac. It will help soothe your nerves. I'm also going to write you one for Zolpidem, which should help regulate your sleep. Then, I want you to make a follow-up appointment with a colleague of mine, Doctor Burke, who specializes in neuroscience. She may be more suited to handle a situation as complex as yours appears. I want you to know that I truly empathize with what you're going through. And if I frustrated you, I apologize. I want nothing more than to see you get the help you need."

"Thanks, Doc. I appreciate your honesty. And I'm sorry too for lashing out. I just want this to end because I can't take it anymore."

"It'll be fine, David. Just take my advice, and I hope everything will work out. Good luck to you."

***

Later that evening, David and Sharon are preparing for bed. The couple is discussing David's session with Doctor Hirshberg. Ever the optimist, Sharon attempts to place her husband's mind at ease.

"Honey, maybe the doctor is right. Maybe there's a simple explanation for what's happening."

"I don't know, Shar. It just doesn't make sense. None of it makes any sense."

As she gently caresses her abdomen, Sharon casts a loving smile in David's direction.

"Well, I know one thing for certain. You and I are the luckiest people alive. This beautiful baby growing inside of me is a blessing. And we're going to be the best parents ever."

David smiles back and wraps his arms tightly around his bride. With a kiss, he says, "I love you, baby. Good night."

"I love you too. Sweet dreams."

***

As the first rays of sunlight pierce through the bedroom blinds, David abruptly wakes in a cold sweat. He tries to catch his breath and regain his composure.

"Holy shit, what an awful dream. Sharon, honey. Wake up. I just had the worst nightmare. We were at the hospital, and you were in labor. It was all fucked up though. So many complications. You gave birth to a baby girl. She was still-born. Then you started to hemorrhage. None of the doctors or nurses could do anything to save you. You bled out right there on the delivery table. It was God-awful."

Placing his hand atop her shoulder, he says, "Sharon, did you hear me? Wake up, baby."

Sharon is stiff and cold to the touch. Her jaw is locked open with rigor. Her face is a ghastly shade of white. David's gift of foreshadowing has once again proved true. With the love of his life and unborn child caught in the firm clutches of death, David is stripped of his last ounce of sanity. Left all alone, his maniacal medley of screams echo throughout the corridors of the home. For David Kovar, the world has become a very empty place.

STRAIGHT TO VOICEMAIL

The Cape Cod-style home sits at the end of a cul-de-sac, flanked by three houses on either side of the street. Cupid's heart, a relic from Valentine's Day six months earlier, still decorates the front door. A tattered American flag hangs to the right of the center awning and drifts lazily in the thick August air. The lawn is dry and patchy. The brutal Indian summer has left it scorched and in desperate need of treatment. A cluster of overgrown bushes creeps well past the large bay window and serves well to mask the emptiness that lies within. The once cozy, inviting confines could have been decorated by Martha Stewart herself. Now, they more closely resemble a frat house, complete with an array of fast-food wrappers and an army of empty Miller Lite cans scattered throughout.

Arthur Johnson and his wife, Colleen, bought the place shortly after they were married five years ago. Arthur is fifteen years her senior and is well-established in his career as a forensic accountant. He is practical and regimented. Everything in his life is in order. Colleen, on the other hand, is more of a free spirit, a true non-conformist. She's held a variety of jobs and is still trying to find herself. Despite being polar opposites, their May/

December romance quickly blossomed. However, their relationship has become tumultuous over the past year. After enduring months of unsuccessful marriage counseling, the two currently find themselves in the midst of a trial separation; divorce is imminent.

But Arthur is not the type of person who can easily embrace change. He's a perfectionist. Failure is not an option. He waited his entire life for a girl like Colleen. He worships her, adores her, and caters to her every need. But everything is different now. His life has been turned upside down. Arthur has lost control and has grown bitter and resentful. For the past three nights, sleep has eluded him. A once sharp mind is now clouded with dark, twisted thoughts. His perpetual state of inebriation only fuels his paranoia.

"Freaking selfish bitch! I loved you so much. Always supported you. And always gave you everything you wanted. And *this* is how you repay me? By walking out and moving back with your parents."

Arthur continues his drinking bender as his thoughts become more toxic.

"My mother told me I was making a mistake. She begged me not to marry you. Said you weren't good enough for me. Said you were going to take me for a ride. 'No way, ma. You don't know Colleen like I do. She'd never do that to me,' I said. What a joke. How wrong was I? She was right all along. You played me for a fool. And I fell for it every step of the way."

Arthur's emotional roller coaster offers him a momentary reprieve from his anger. He smiles and reminisces as he uses his phone to scroll through pictures of him and Colleen from a trip to Aruba.

"Look how happy we were. Not a care in the world. But look at us now!"

However, the moment is short-lived. Happiness fades and turns to rage. Arthur erupts and launches the phone across the room. It smashes against the wall, shattering into pieces.

"Hahaha. What a mess. Just like our relationship. One big, unrecognizable mess. Fuck this. It doesn't even matter. Nothing matters anymore."

Arthur has decided to take back control. He's always lived his life on his own terms. It's only fitting that he will end his life on his own terms as well.

After a trip to his garage, Arthur returns to his living room with a heavy, orange extension cord. He ties it around the top of the banister and loops it several more times until he achieves the necessary height. The oak railing is more than sturdy enough to support his weight. He rigs the other end into a make-shift noose and fits it snugly around his neck. The coffee table is wobbly. He struggles to steady himself.

"I hope you're happy, baby. You drove me to this."

He inches closer to the edge of the table. His heart races. His palms are sweaty. His legs begin to shake. Arthur is tired and alone. He takes another choppy step forward and inhales ever so slightly. His eyes are closed. He has accepted his fate. But then, an obnoxious, blaring noise. Of all things, his landline telephone.

RING, RING, RING, RING

Arthur tries to re-focus himself to the task at hand. But the incessant ringing continues.

RING, RING, RING, RING

Until it stops.

BEEP

The soothingly familiar voice on the other end sends Arthur into a trance.

"Honey, it's me, Colleen. Listen, I...I'm sorry. I want to come home. I don't know what I was thinking. I guess my insecurities got the best of me. This is so hard for me to admit, but deep down, I never thought I was good enough for you. I mean, you're so confident and successful. Everything in your life is just the way you want it. And me? I feel like I'm all over the place, like I can never get my act together. I just got overwhelmed, baby. That's all. I know that's no excuse for leaving. I never should've walked away from you like that. You're the best thing that ever happened to me, and I promise I will never, ever hurt you again. I miss you, Artie. You know, it's funny. I feel so stupid talking to a machine. I called your cell, but it must be off. It just went straight to voicemail. Anyway, I'm on my way home, baby. I'll see you in a bit. I love you."

BEEP

A gentle sigh seeps from Arthur's quivering lips as his body drifts into a state of relaxed calm. The moment is surreal, and he wonders if he's dreaming. But, no. This isn't a dream. This is real. After six excruciatingly painful months alone, Colleen, the love of his life, is coming home.

"I love you too, sweetheart. I prayed every day that God would bring you back to me. He finally answered my prayers."

As he surveys the room, Arthur's euphoria disappears and is replaced by slight panic.

"Christ, this place is a disaster. I have to straighten up before Colleen gets home. Everything has to be perfect. And there isn't much time. I have to hurry."

With a sense of urgency, Arthur takes a giant step forward.

REDEMPTION

Car Ride to Upstate New York - Sunday, October 12, 2003

"Where the fuck is this place? We've been driving all fucking day."

"We have about an hour to go. Please try to be patient, baby. And I really wish you wouldn't swear like that, Ric. It makes me uncomfortable."

"Another fucking hour! Christ almighty. This is fucking bullshit in the first place. I did my job. I was a good fucking cop. Did everything those blow jobs asked me to do and more. And this is how they repay me."

"Are you kidding me right now, Ric? You're lucky you're not in jail. You should have been indicted. This is an absolute blessing that we're able to start over. Not many people get a second chance in life. My Uncle Ray's generosity is a godsend. He's opened his arms and his heart to us. He is a pious and forgiving man with infinite wisdom. I want you to learn from him, darling. We can live in peace and tranquility in this beautiful land where I grew up. Be grateful, Ric, please. Like I said, not many people get second chances like this."

"Yeah, some second chance. Banished to some back-woods, shithole town upstate. A million miles from any-thing. Punished like some freaking criminal. Just like the garbage I picked up off the streets for all those years. Bottom line, I got shit *done*. Who gives a fuck how I did it!"

"Again with cursing. Honey, you did some really bad things. But it's not too late for you to be a righteous man. You can redeem yourself. I'm here to help you with that. Please, baby, let's embrace this opportunity and make the most of our new life together."

"Whose side are you on for Chrissake? I did what I had to do. And stop lecturing me about my fucking mouth. You knew who I was when you married me. I'll curse as much as I fucking want to!"

Cindi just shakes her head. A lone tear descends the curvature of her flawless cheek bone. At the same time, Ric lets out a long sigh and gazes zombie-like out the window, watching the endless array of rolling pastures. There's nothing more for as far as the eye can see.

His mind drifts off to the place and time when he first met Cindi. It was only two years ago – Bryant Park in downtown Manhattan. At the time, Ric Martino had just been promoted to Detective First Grade in the NYPD and was assigned to the street crimes narcotics unit. He was an aggressive, proactive cop, who led the department in arrests and successful prosecutions for three straight years. He was a highly decorated and well-respected officer who wasn't influenced or intimidated by the New York City political machine.

Like many of his testosterone-filled, type-A coworkers, Ric's appetite for vigilant police work was surpassed only by his appetite for sex. An extremely handsome man, he never had any trouble attracting the ladies. His arrogance and misogynistic ways didn't seem to stifle his efforts in the least. Over the years, Ric had an array of beautiful women at his side. When he locked eyes with

Cindi that evening, he was instantly mesmerized. She was stunning. A statuesque, raven-haired beauty more suited for the arm of an A-list celebrity than for a salty NYPD detective. Cindi was different from all his other conquests. She was truly virtuous. Ric didn't deserve her, and he knew it. Yet he still pursued her, knowing full well she was far out of his league.

Cindi was only twenty-two at the time, ten years younger than Ric. She was new to the bar scene in Manhattan. In fact, she was new to the entire area. She grew up in the Village of Moravia, New York. Just shy of 300 miles from New York City, Moravia is nestled in the middle of Cayuga County – a tiny hamlet wedged between the Canadian border and northwestern Pennsylvania. Cindi may as well have told Ric she was from the planet Mars because it was all the same to him. He knew nothing of life outside the five boroughs that make up New York City – the place he was born and raised. The gritty virtues of the city not only fit Ric's character perfectly, but they also define him. It is where he belongs. He is boorish and crude. The opposite of Cindi. Her mere presence exudes class, elegance, and an innocence seldom seen in New York City culture. She came to the city to find herself. She begged her Uncle Ray, the man who raised her, for permission to go. Cindi told him she wanted to help others who were lost and in need of guidance. No one in Cindi's family had ever dared to leave the safe confines of Cayuga County. And why would they? Considered nature's paradise, the area is pure and untouched. When Cindi met Ric, she knew he needed saving more than anyone she had ever encountered. She just didn't know the full extent of it.

Flashback - Brooklyn, NY - Bedford Stuyvesant Section - Monday, October 6

"This is it."

"You sure?"

"Yeah, I'm fucking sure. I went over this with my informant a hundred times. He said it's 1044 Monroe Street. Two houses down from the park. He knows his shit. He's always delivered for me in the past. He's not gonna fuck me on this one."

"All right, Ric, all right. I'll trust you. But if you're wrong, this is gonna be a total shit storm. I'm telling you right now I'm not going down for this. You own it."

"Yeah, yeah. I own it. Whatever. It's legit. The dude goes by the name of 'Kiki.' And every fucking Thursday he drops off a major delivery of blow, weed, pills, *everything* to that fucking house just in time for the weekend push. I'm telling you. It's a done deal. Nothing's gonna happen."

Ric and his lieutenant, Michael Dammann, are sitting in an unmarked Crown Victoria in the parking lot of Kennedy Fried Chicken, directly across from Raymond Bush Playground. Another unit is positioned on the corner of Throop Avenue and Monroe Street. The other members of the "take down" team are scattered around the entire perimeter of the target house– two cars on Madison Street and two on Marcus Garvey Boulevard. Once inside the perimeter, Kiki will have nowhere to run.

Raymond Bush Playground - 11:30 a.m.

A Nissan Maxima with tinted windows rolls to a stop directly in front of Raymond Bush Playground, the park near the target house. A tall, thinly built black male steps out from the front passenger side. He has shoulder-length dreadlocks and is wearing a black hoodie with gray sweatpants. He glances cautiously down both ends of the street.

In his left hand, he carries a black backpack. His right hand is concealed in the front pocket of his sweatshirt. He slowly takes his first steps away from the vehicle and toward the park. But he suddenly stops, like a nervous gazelle, sensing something just isn't right.

Realizing the cover has been blown, Ric gives the command over the radio.

"Move in! Take him down!"

With tires screeching, Ric jumps the curb and angle blocks the Nissan, pinning it curbside. In an instant, he is out of the car and in pursuit of Kiki, who by now is in full stride running straight toward the park, still clutching his bag.

"Police. You better fucking stop!"

Hearing this command, Kiki turns and blades his body toward Ric, his right hand now exposed.

Ric shouts, "Gun!" and sends a volley of .40 caliber rounds screaming toward Kiki.

Two rounds connect center mass and drop Kiki into a crumpled heap at the foot of the park's entrance. The next round lodges itself into an oak tree inside the park. The last round goes rogue and strikes a woman in the head while she waits for an MTA bus on the corner of Marcus Garvey Boulevard and Monroe Street.

The echoes of gunshots fade and give way to the new sounds of panicked pedestrian screams and ear-piercing police sirens converging on the scene.

With his Glock still trained on the lifeless body, Ric stands over Kiki and stares blindly in disbelief. In just under thirty seconds, Ric had taken two lives and had changed his own life forever.

The bag Kiki had been clutching now lies at his side, its contents exposed for the first time: a brand-new pair of Nike Air Flightposite basketball sneakers, the same kind worn by NBA stars Tim Duncan and Kevin Garnett. His right hand is frozen in a death grip on a cell phone.

Despite the chaos, the faint voice of an NYPD dispatcher can still be heard on speaker mode.

"9-1-1, where is your emergency?"

"Kiki's" real name is LaDonne Taylor. His close friends call him L.T. He is a seventeen-year-old senior at the Bedford Stuyvesant Preparatory High School, just two blocks away. On this particular day, all New York City public schools were closed for the observance of the Jewish holiday of Yom Kippur. Thus, LaDonne was meeting friends that morning for some pick-up basketball at the park. Those Flights were his most prized possession. He worked as a server at a local Applebee's and had saved the entire summer for those kicks. He had been certain that he was about to get jumped and robbed. That's why LaDonne ran. That's why he dialed 9-1-1, just like his mom told him to do if he was ever in danger.

His mom, Trisha Sampson, had parked her Nissan Maxima curbside to drop LaDonne off at Raymond Bush Park, like she had done so many times in the past. Only this time, instead of watching her only son sink three-point shots, she watched as he was executed in one of the grossest cases of mistaken identity in the history of law enforcement.

Amid the chaos and confusion, a dark-colored Nissan Maxima slowly rolls by the intersection of Throop Avenue and Monroe Street, which is now completely cordoned off by emergency vehicles. The tinted passenger side window cracks open and exposes a black male with shoulder length dreads. His eyes dart nervously back and forth, surveying the scene of carnage.

As he inconspicuously drives off, unnoticed by Ric or any of the other team members, Kiki says to himself, "Damn, I'm one lucky nigga."

The political fallout from this tragedy nearly cripples the NYPD and the city of New York. Racial tensions between blacks and whites are already high. The growing distrust of the police in many of the minority communities continues to fester. Community activists and anti-police groups work together in concert to call for the indictment of Ric Martino and the resignation of most of the upper echelon of the NYPD. Protests are held outside of 1 Police Plaza and throughout many precincts in all five boroughs. The public demonstrations, the constant barrage of the media, and the inevitable lawsuits finally force the hand of the police administration. Ric has become a political pawn in a city on the verge of collapse. He is given two choices, neither of which appeals to him. He is either going to be indicted and formally charged in the wrongful death of two innocent civilians, or he is going to take advantage of his wife's connections and transfer in the utmost secrecy to obscurity and anonymity. Ric Martino reluctantly and bitterly chooses the latter.

Present Day - Sunday, October 12

Ric and Cindi arrive in Cayuga County and meet Cindi's Uncle Raymond Lehigh, sheriff of Cayuga County. As their car pulls up to the Cayuga County Sheriff's Office, Ric thinks to himself that perhaps he would have been better off if he had rolled the dice and taken his chances with the indictment. With Cindi by his side, Ric finally comes face-to-face for the first time with her beloved uncle.

As she runs into his waiting arms, she says, "Uncle Ray!"

In a loving embrace, her uncle warmly acknowledges her.

"My sweet child. It is so good to have you back home where you belong. You have been missed dearly."

Raymond Lehigh is a formidable man in both stature and aura. Standing 6 feet 6 inches tall with shoulders as broad as the Colorado Rockies, his mere presence is intimidating yet captivating at the same time. His perfectly coiffed salt and pepper hair complements his olive complexion. Sharp facial features and flawless skin tone suggest he is much younger than his actual age. His piercing green eyes tell the story of a worldly man, well steeped with adventures and wisdom.

With both hands extended, speaking in an inviting voice, he cordially greets his new visitor.

"You must be Ric. Welcome to Cayuga, my friend. We welcome you. We embrace you. We open our land to you. Take solace in knowing that we are a forgiving people who do not judge. We only ask that you respect our values and our way of life. Redemption is yours if you so seek it. Thus, your eternity of salvation awaits."

Instinctively sizing up the man he has heard so much about, Ric turns his head toward Cindi.

"Holy shit, babe. You didn't tell me your uncle was a sheriff *and* a preacher."

Ric continues, "Let me tell you something, *Uncle Ray*. I agreed to come to this town because they had me by the balls back home. Believe me, it wasn't by choice. Now, don't get me wrong. I appreciate the job offer. But I'll be damned if I'm gonna listen to a lecture on morality and forgiveness from a guy who walks around like his shit doesn't stink."

"Your arrogance offends me, as does your foul mouth. My beloved niece always looks for the good in people. She has assured me there is good inside of you. Do not make a liar out of her and a fool of me. As I said, Ric, embrace our culture. Respect our values. Learn to appreciate life, and you will find a home here. Now take some time to look around our village. Educate yourself about our people and our way of life. My deputy will take you to your quarters."

As he leaves, Sheriff Lehigh kisses Cindi on the cheek and whispers something in her ear. He then returns to his office and closes the door.

Alone with Cindi, Ric mocks the man for his candor.

"Is that freaking guy for real? People? Way of life? What the hell was that old screwball talking about?"

"Please watch your mouth, Ric. And don't be so disrespectful to my uncle. He doesn't deserve to be talked to like that. And for the record, he's talking about the Iroquois Nation. Those are *our* people, *our* tribe."

"Wait a minute. Wait a freaking minute. You told me you were part fucking Cherokee or some shit like that. What the hell is an Iroquois?"

"There are five Nations that make up the League of Iroquois: Mohawk, Oneida, Onondaga, Seneca, and Cayuga. I told you on the night we first met that I was full-blooded Iroquois. I told you that, Ric. You were either too drunk or too consumed in your own ego to pay much attention. Like Uncle Ray said, the Iroquois people are a generous group who are here to help you. Help you find your salvation. I'm here to guide you. That's why we met that night. The gods brought us together. You need saving, Ric. Let me show you the way."

"The only thing I need saving from, doll, is this nightmare I'm stuck in. I can't believe this shit is happening to me. It keeps getting better and better."

At this time, Deputy Warren Hightower appears and is ready to show Ric and Cindi their lodging.

"Whoa. Here comes Barney Fife. You here to take us to Aunt Bee's house?"

Either the Andy Griffith Show reference went over his head or he just chose to ignore the insult. Either way, Deputy Hightower promptly and without a word escorts Ric and Cindi to an apartment directly behind the municipal building.

"Hey, Barney, why don't you make yourself useful and point me in the direction of your local watering hole. I'm gonna need some serious booze to deal with this debacle."

"Cayuga County is a dry county. You will find no such libations here, sir."

"You have *got* to be shitting me? Un-fucking-believable! How in the holy hell am I supposed to cope with everything that's going on if I can't even catch a buzz? I mean this *can't* be real. Where the hell am I?"

Cindi tries her best to settle him down.

"Ric, baby. Calm yourself. Let's take a walk, and I'll show you around. You'll see the beauty in all. Your eyes and soul will be opened. You won't need any alcohol. You will be high on nature. Trust me."

"Fuck my life," Ric mumbles as he follows Cindi out the door.

Cayuga County Sheriff's Office - Monday, October 13, 8:00 a.m.

The next morning, with Cindi at his side for moral support, Ric reports to work for his new assignment as a deputy for the Cayuga County Sheriff's Office. He is met by Sheriff Lehigh and Deputy Hightower. Always poised and professional, Sheriff Lehigh greets Ric.

"Good morning, my friend. I trust you found your new accommodations pleasant. This is a new day. Like every other new day in Cayuga, we welcome it and give thanks to our gods who bestowed it upon us. For the time being, you will be working with Deputy Hightower. He will be training you in our methods and ideologies. He is an excellent role model, who has a wealth of knowledge and is well steeped in Cayuga history and culture. Please learn from him, as he will set a good example."

"Did you say this ass clown will be training me?

Taking a deep breath, Sheriff Lehigh calmly reiterates his message.

"Yes, Ric. That is correct. Deputy Hightower will be your training officer. You should model yourself after him."

"Model myself after *him*?" Let me tell you something, pal. I got fifteen years on the job with the NYPD. In case you didn't understand me, let me spell that for you. N-Y-P-D. You know what that means? It means we're the best. We've got the best training. We've got the best equipment. We work in the best city. We perform the best police work. We've got the best of *everything*! You can't teach me a goddamn thing about police work that I don't already know."

"I see the quiet time you spent with my niece did not clear your head at all. Your clouded vision and impure thoughts still consume you. Once again, you have insulted Cayuga, our people, and our way of life. You continue to disappoint me, Ric. I pray that you find your way sooner rather than later."

Uncle Ray whispers in Cindi's ear and gives Deputy Hightower a nod.

"He's all yours, Deputy."

Begrudgingly, Ric spends his first week in training under Deputy Hightower. Much of the day is spent trolling leisurely through the wooded sprawl of the county. Ric sits back silently as Deputy Hightower drones on about Iroquois culture and how important and revered it is. There is not a single call for service. No reported crimes. No speeders or other moving violations. There is not even so much as a simple parking infraction.

On Friday, October 17, Deputy Hightower shows Ric the evidence room. As Ric starts sifting through old records and case files, he discovers a disturbing trend: an inordinate amount of missing persons cases. The deputy continues to ramble on about administrative functions and records bureau protocol, but Ric abruptly interrupts.

"What's the deal with all these missing persons cases?"

"Do not concern yourself with those." Further trying to divert the question, he says, "They are very old cases that have been closed."

"See, that's exactly what I'm talking about. You freaking backwoods hillbillies don't know the first thing about police work. Missing persons cases are *never* administratively closed out. They remain open until the victim is either located or confirmed deceased."

Leaving Deputy Hightower at a loss for words, Ric continues his berating.

"Deputy, you would fuck up a wet dream. You're so far over your head it's not even funny. I mean look at this shit. There's got to be at least a dozen jackets here going back to the '60's for Chrissake. How is it possible so many people go reported missing? Nobody's working any leads? Nobody noticed any trends? Doesn't it seem odd to you, Deputy, that nobody even jay-walks in your precious little utopia here? Yet half the freaking population just up and vanishes without a trace. And this pompous imbecile sheriff of yours is letting it happen. What the fuck are you doing up here, bro?"

As Ric looks up, he discovers Sheriff Lehigh staring sternly down at him. Cindi is also at her uncle's side.

"Oh, hello there, *Sheriff*. I was just talking about you. You know, Sheriff, for someone who is so thorough and insistent when it comes to following the rules and acting appropriately, I'm shocked at the absurd amount of unsolved missing persons cases you have under your jurisdiction. Talk about a farce. You parade yourself around like some freaking messiah with everybody kissing your ass. Everybody in this shithole town is brainwashed, including my wife. You're like the modern-day Jim Jones. Don't drink the Kool-Aid, man! You pretend to know everything, trying to intimidate people by using big, fancy words and quoting scripture when you really don't know shit. You got all these missing persons cases on your shelves collecting dust, and you're afraid to look into them? Either that or you're too inept to even try. And even though you like to think you're above me, we're identical in one aspect. You and I took the same oath. You swore to uphold the law just like I did. You talk about me disrespecting your culture? Well, let me tell you something. You're disrespecting that badge, those people who are still missing, and their families! I may be a lot of things, some good and some not so good, but I'm a hell of a cop. It's in my blood. And I'm gonna show you just how good my instincts are. I'm gonna work these cases and solve them. Yeah, that's what I'm gonna do. And guess what. That's gonna be my ticket out of here. I'll give closure to the families, get my boy at the *New York Post* to do a story on it, and ride the glory wave all the way back to the NYPD, where I belong. They'll realize what a great fucking cop I am and how big a mistake it was to let me go in the first place. I'll be reinstated as a detective first grade and get my shield back. No doubt."

Turning his attention to Cindi, he says, "Maybe then, doll, you'll come to your senses and listen to me again instead of following this snake oil salesman."

Sheriff Lehigh says not one word. Instead, he slowly turns toward Cindi, whispers something in her ear, and leaves her alone in the room with Ric. The couple stare at each other briefly until Ric finally explodes.

"What! Don't just stand there like a deer in the headlights. Spit it out."

"There's nothing more I can say, Ric. I've said it all to no avail."

"Stop with the holier-than-thou crap. That routine is getting old already. Your uncle is pissed off because I called him out on his bullshit. And he's not used to that. I'm sure nobody's ever stood up to him before. Well, that's too goddamn bad. Poor Uncle Ray got caught with his pants down and his dick floppin' in the wind. He didn't say anything because he couldn't. He knows I'm right. I got him. I know his game. His house of cards just came crashing down, sweetheart, and he's panicking. If he didn't have his head so far up his own ass, then maybe he'd realize how fucked up this really is."

"You're so crude."

"Yeah, that's right. I am crude. But I'm real, unlike your uncle. He's a phony. Him and his whole police department. The first cases involving actual police work and they wanna cover them up like they never existed. All because they don't know what the hell they're doing. Well, that's a fucking travesty. They're afraid of being exposed for who they really are, a bunch of ass-backward wanna-be cops in a no-nothing town. And you go right along with it, brainwashed like a lackey, buying into all this nonsense. Well, not me, honey. Ric Martino is nobody's bitch. And like I said to him, I'm still gonna find out what happened to those poor schleps so I can get the hell outta here. I'm also gonna prove to you that your uncle is connected somehow. Then maybe you'll come back to reality, doll, and know your role."

With that, Cindi walks silently out of the room, as Ric finishes his tirade with parting sarcasm.

"Thanks for standing by your man, baby. Pathetic."

***

Ric spends the better part of the following week reviewing the case files and doing research. He attempts to locate any witnesses. He tries contacting surviving family members or friends of the missing. He looks for past employers and coworkers. He speaks with members of the community. He checks hospital records in the surrounding areas during the time periods in question. However, he develops not a single lead.

On Friday at the end of the workday, Ric finds himself buried in a mountain of paperwork including old case files, statements, and the like. As his frustration grows, he realizes he is at a standstill, unable to make any progress in his quest to uncover the truth behind the disappearances. Ric's mind wanders. He begins to ponder his fate, his relationship with Cindi, and his future in general. As he becomes overwhelmed with clouded thoughts, the office door bursts open. It is Cindi, crying hysterically.

"You're right, baby. You're right. My uncle is involved. I didn't want to believe it, but it's true."

Jumping up out of his seat, Ric inquires, "What happened?"

"I can't, baby. I can't even begin to explain to you."

"What happened, damn it?"

"It's just too much. I can't. Oh my God."

"Okay, where is he? Where's your uncle?"

"He's down by the lake. I just left him. Ran out of there as quick as I could to find you. I'm so sorry for doubting you, Ric. Will you ever forgive me?"

"Yeah, babe. I'll forgive you. You can make it up to me later tonight if you know what I mean. But first, I'm gonna deal with your precious uncle and put an end to this charade once and for all. Let's go."

Cindi leads Ric down to the mouth of Lake Ontario, where they find Sheriff Lehigh standing alone, staring out at the lake, under a perfectly calm moonlit night.

Unable to control his fury, Ric erupts.

"Time's up, asshole. You got nowhere else to run. I know there's a cover-up, and I know you're behind it. Come clean already. Tell me what you told my wife to get her so upset. Admit to me that you had something to do with those missing persons. I told you before I was gonna get to the bottom of this. Did you really think you were gonna get one over on me, Sheriff? I'm a first grade detective for the New York City Police Department. Nobody gets one over on Ric Martino. Now, once and for all, tell me what the fuck is going on."

Sheriff Lehigh breaks his silence.

"Welcome, Ric. I'm so glad you're here. And you are correct. I *did* underestimate you. You *are* an outstanding detective with great natural instincts."

"Stop stroking me already and get to the point. And goddamn it, turn around and face me like a man when I'm talking to you!"

"As you wish."

Sheriff Lehigh slowly and methodically turns and is now face-to-face with Ric. He locks eyes with him and continues to speak.

"When I first met you a week ago, I welcomed you to our land. I told you that you had a home here in Cayuga County. I asked you to embrace our culture and respect our values. And although it was against my better judgment, I trusted my niece when she told me deep down you were a good man."

He pauses and then bellows in a booming voice of mythical proportions.

"You have done nothing but disrespect and desecrate our way of life!"

Visibly shaken by the thunderous proclamation, Ric attempts to regain his composure. However, he appears to be in a trance-like state, cowering like an anxious child awaiting punishment.

"You want to know the truth? So it be said. I am Orenda, the creator. I am the high God of the Iroquois Nation."

Ric watches in horror as Orenda levitates. His arms extend and grow to ten feet in length. A glowing orange flame illuminates his figure. For the first time in his life, Ric Martino experiences bone-chilling fear.

Desperately trying to awaken from this nightmare, Ric screams, "Baby! What the hell is going on! Help me!"

In a somber voice, Cindi replies, "I tried to help you, Ric. That's all I ever wanted to do. I stood by your side for the past two years, hoping you would open your eyes. I tried to give you the power necessary to bring you to a spiritual place where we could both remain eternal to each other. You ignored my attempts to guide you. You mocked me. You laughed at my traditions. Did you think it was a mere coincidence we found each other, my dear? No, Ric. There are no such things as coincidences. It was fate that brought us together. I looked down upon you and saw you struggling. Saw this lost soul in need of help.

I descended from the heavens to heal you in every way possible. For I am Skywoman, the Mother Goddess of Cayuga. I thought this time was different, Ric. I thought *you* were different. But I was wrong. You proved to be just like all the men who came before you. The men who also needed saving. Those names on the police reports. They, too, neglected my efforts and ignored my nurturing ways. My attempts to show them the true light of salvation went unanswered. Alas, you, too, have failed me, Ric. And thus, I have also failed you."

With those words, Skywoman launches herself upward, high into the midnight sky. In stunned disbelief, Ric watches as a giant hole in the sky opens and envelopes his beloved Cindi.

Lake Ontario is now engulfed in flames. The beleaguered and tortured spirits of Cayuga mythology all reveal themselves to Ric:

The Stone Throwers – dwarf-like creatures – run rampant and chant in tongues.

The Stone Coats – giants with skin as hard as bedrock – lumber with an incandescent glow.

Naked Bear – an enormous, hairless creature resembling a mammoth – lurches about uprooting tree stumps and boulders.

Flying Head – a monster in the form of a giant disembodied head – menacingly circles the sky.

Dry Fingers – a disembodied mummified arm – glides through the night and grasps at anything in its path.

The surreal circus of biblical carnage proves too much for any man to endure, even Ric Martino. All his bravado, all his confidence, all his courage instantly drains from his body. Ric could do nothing to stop the utter madness that unfolded before him. Falling to his knees and sobbing uncontrollably, Ric begs The Creator for forgiveness.

"*Now* you ask to be forgiven? It is too late," declares The Creator. "Forgiveness is a luxury granted to those worthy and appreciative enough to receive it. You, Ric, have proved yourself otherwise. Your purpose here was simple: assimilate to our culture. If you'd done so, you would have been granted your forgiveness and the reward of immortality. Now, you will receive a different type of reward, that of soul cleansing. And the only way to truly wash one's spirit is to give oneself to the mighty Onyare."

As if on cue, the waters of Lake Ontario begin to part. From the depths of the great abyss rises a prehistoric reptilian behemoth nearly three stories tall. The Great Onyare, a tri-horned dragon-like serpent of the Great Lakes, emerges with a furious, ear-shattering shriek. The guttural howl is heard for miles throughout the Villages of Cayuga County. The town elders are all too familiar with what is to follow.

In a futile attempt to prolong the inevitable, Ric tries to escape by frantically running and looking for a place to hide. However, with lightening-like precision, Onyare's slime-covered claw snatches him up while he is in mid-stride.

Upside down, Ric dangles precariously in the grip of the massive beast. In hysterics, he stares directly into the gapping mouth of the great serpent. Although Onyare's venomous breath nearly causes him to pass out, Ric remains lucid enough to look passed the puss-covered jowls and discovers an irony large enough to choke a horse.

In his quest for the truth, Ric Martino has solved his final case. As Onyare lets go of him, Ric descends into the cavernous depths of the beast's belly. The last image Ric sees is that of the twelve missing men. Their faces ghastly. Their bodies contorted. Their souls lost. Ric Martino now joins them and dances in a pit of fire for all eternity.

Midtown Manhattan - Port Authority Bus Terminal

The familiar sound of squeaking airbrakes from the Greyhound bus indicates it has arrived at its destination. As the passengers descend the platform to embark on their journeys, they move like cattle and blend seamlessly into the drab urban landscape. One passenger, however, stands out from the rest of the herd. Although she has been to the city in this same exact place countless times in the past, she pauses to take in her surroundings as if it were her first time. She is a statuesque, raven-haired beauty. Her name is Cindi.

SISTER, SISTER

"Oh my God, I'm so nervous. I can't believe this day is finally here. Even though we've had our differences, if it wasn't for you, my sister, I wouldn't be standing here, in this beautiful dress. You've always been there for me. And I promise I'll be there for you when it's your turn."

Rachel always knew she would walk down the aisle one day. However, she never dreamed it would happen *before* it happened for her older sister, Julie.

The girls are only sixteen months apart. However, from her earliest recollection, Rachel has always lived in Julie's shadow. Julie learned to ride a bike first. Her clothing was passed down to Rachel as second hand. She earned better grades than Rachel. Julie was permitted to date first. And thus, her curfew was later. She was a high school cheerleader, while Rachel played in the marching band. Julie, a college graduate, has a high-paying job. Rachel earns a meager living waiting tables at a local diner.

"I know it must be awkward for you. Truth be told, it's a little weird for me too, all things considered. After all, you and Brian dated for three years. Everyone just assumed you'd be getting married. Even I came to terms with that. But looking back, it was clear you weren't right for each other. Maybe you just grew apart. I don't know. Either way, he was completely devastated after the break-up. I was only trying to console him. He needed someone to talk to, and I just happened to be there to listen. But I swear to you, I never expected anything to happen between us. Crazy as it sounds, I think you and I have grown closer because of this. It's a true testament to our sisterly bond that we can both be adults and accept the fact that *I'm* the one marrying Brian."

In Rachel's eyes, Julie has always been her parent's favorite. They spoiled her rotten and constantly doted on her. At one point, they even bought her a snow globe that read "#1 Daughter." To this day, Julie keeps it on her dresser as a fond reminder of her childhood. For Rachel, the memories are not as warm and fuzzy.

"I know what you're thinking. This wedding came as a shock to everyone, most of all Mom and Dad. Let's face it, you were always their favorite. They catered to you, while I got stuck with your leftovers. Being the runner-up all the time gets old. Trust me, it's not much fun. But all that has changed now. This is *my* day. Yours will come. But this one belongs to me."

The bride-to-be stares blissfully into the full-length cheval mirror. The image staring back nearly brings a tear to her eye. Perfect hair. Flawless makeup. Her form-fitting dress, long and flowing, gives her the seductive elegance of a Hollywood starlet. Her parents and other relatives are downstairs in the living room, eagerly awaiting her arrival. The limousine is idling in front of their house. In the distance, church bells toll.

Her trance is broken by the sound of her father's voice.

"Honey, let's go. You're going to be late."

It's time. My time.

"I love you, sister. Always have. Always will."

Like a princess in a fairytale, she slowly descends the staircase to her waiting subjects.

Look how they stare at me, marveling at my beauty. How utterly perfect.

However, the puzzled looks on their faces tell a different story.

Again, her father's voice fills the air.

"What the hell are you doing, *Rachel*? Where's Julie?"

Her dad rushes past her and scales the stairs, two at a time. Moments later, shrieks of terror reverberate throughout the home.

"Julie! My God, Julie!"

In shock, the patriarch cradles the lifeless body of his first-born daughter, her bloodied head nestled in his arms.

***

Dressed only in her bridal undergarments, Julie relaxes as her younger sister brushes her long, golden hair. She admires her wedding dress, as it hangs on the back of the closet door. While pampering her older sister, Rachel reaches behind her and picks up the item that came to epitomize her childhood. Wearing the smile of the Cheshire Cat, Rachel will no longer settle for second place.

The first blow renders Julie unconscious. The subsequent twenty-three cave in her skull, transforming it into an unrecognizable piece of chop meat. The encore of Rachel's ghoulish crescendo consists of a singular note, in the form of a loud thud. She watches as the snow globe, now a fierce shade of crimson, rolls across the bedroom floor. Notwithstanding the matted hair and brain matter, the words "#1 Daughter" are still somewhat visible.

***

The hysteria is contagious. The smell of death lingers in the warm summer air. Bathed in the flesh and blood of her own sister, Rachel walks into the kitchen and pours herself a mimosa. As she raises the delicate flute to her blood-stained lips, she is suddenly overcome by a strange feeling. However, it is not one of remorse or regret. Instead, Rachel has a classic case of the wedding day jitters. Her mind begins to race with second thoughts.

This is such a huge commitment, certainly not to be taken lightly. After all, marriage is forever. The more I think about it, Brian and I really don't know each other all that well. Maybe this is a mistake. Yes, it's one big mistake. Great. Now, what am I going to do? So many of our friends and relatives traveled to see me. All the time and effort in planning. Not to mention Mom and Dad spent a fortune on the reception. They're going to be so disappointed. Think, Rachel. Think. You must do something to fix this. Wait a minute. Of course, that's it. Julie should marry Brian. They're perfect for each other. I can't wait to tell her the good news. She's going to be so excited. Plus, she's going to make a beautiful bride.

"Julie. Julie, where are you? This is the biggest day of your life, and I'm so happy for you, my sister. But there's so much to do with so little time. Good thing I'm here to help you get ready. Now, let's get started.

First, we'll do your hair and then your makeup. And that dress. It's absolutely to die for. In fact, I would literally *kill* to wear a dress like that someday!

COVER CHARGE

Club Nitro, Manasquan, New Jersey

During the summer, the club scene at the Jersey Shore has always been the premier place to party. From Point Pleasant Beach to Seaside Heights, this eleven-mile stretch of coastline is littered with some of the hottest clubs in the entire state. Every night, these establishments are filled to capacity with hedonistic young adults in search of non-stop ecstasy. The overflow of testosterone and estrogen combine to form the perfect catalyst for lust-filled encounters on a nightly basis. Nineteen-year-old Tiffany Andiloro and her twenty-year-old friend Jacqueline Buscaino, are about to be indoctrinated into this exclusive scene for the first time.

"I'm telling you, Tiff, this is the hottest club in the area. Everyone goes to Nitro."

"I don't know, Jackie. I'm nervous. What if I don't get in?"

"Are you kidding me? You're gonna get in. The fake ID Tony made you is mint. Nobody's gonna question it."

"Are you sure? I mean, I got kicked out of Surf Club in Seaside two weeks ago. There were like a hundred people in line just staring and laughing at me. I was mortified."

"The hell with Surf Club. That place is beat anyway. Plus, you had that shitty ID your sister used years ago. It's cheap as hell. And the picture doesn't even look like you. What did you expect?"

"I know, but still. I think this might be the same bouncer. He looks like him at least."

"Why? Because he's a big bald guy on steroids? Please. Even if it *is* him, these bouncers see hundreds of people a night. He's not even gonna remember you."

"Fine. If you say so."

After thirty minutes of waiting, Tiffany and Jacqueline edge closer to the front of the line. As her anxiety mounts, Tiffany pleads her case one last time.

"Jackie, maybe this isn't such a good idea. Let's just go. I can call my sister to pick us up."

"Are you friggin' kidding me? We're literally next in line. We're not going anywhere."

"Jackie, I'm just really nervous. I have a weird feeling about all this."

"Jesus, Tiffany. You need to relax. You're drawing attention to us. You're gonna screw everything up!"

"Yelling at me isn't making this any better. You're supposed to be my friend."

"I am your friend. And I'm sorry for getting upset with you. But you need to listen to me. *Nothing* is going to happen. I promise. I just really want to get in here tonight. Paulie's gonna be here. And he's bringing his cousin Mark."

"He's bringing Mark?"

"Yup."

"Is this the same Mark who was with Paulie at the Italian Festival in Hoboken last weekend?"

"Mm-hmm."

"The one with the tattoos who was driving the white Lexus?"

"That's the one."

"OMG, he's really cute."

"I know. And he's totally into you."

"Shut up."

"I'm serious. Paulie told me so. Now, if you play your cards right, he's all yours. Once we get inside, you're gonna realize how silly it was that you were ever scared in the first place. Don't you trust me?"

Before Tiffany has a chance to respond to Jacqueline's loaded question, she is startled by the deep voice of the man working the door.

"ID."

Tiffany looks up at the hulking figure who towers over her petite frame. Reluctantly, she gives him what he's looking for. His gargantuan hands envelop the flimsy piece of laminate. He studies it carefully, then stares back at the frightened girl. Although it seems like an eternity, the entire process takes only a few seconds.

"Go ahead," he grunts.

Before Tiffany can speak, Jacqueline swiftly pushes her friend through the threshold and into the club. She then undergoes the same scrutiny from the bouncer, before successfully joining Tiffany on the inside.

"You see, girl? No big deal. I told you that you had nothing to worry about."

"Yeah, I guess you were right. I know it's stupid, but I just get anxious. That's all."

"It's okay. I get it. Let's just get a drink. It'll help you relax."

"I can definitely use a drink. Then let's find Mark and Paulie and really have some fun."

"Yes! That's the Tiffany I know. I have a feeling this is going to a night we're never gonna forget. Remember, like I always say, what's the worst that can happen?"

With drinks in hand, Jackie and Tiffany make their way through the crowd and onto the dance floor. The steady base pulses through the sound system, vibrating the entire room, which is filled with overly muscular men peacocking in attempts to gain the attention of their female counterparts. In this sea of orgiastic young adults, one particular club-goer seems oddly out of place. This man is not smiling, nor frowning. He stares blankly, showing no interest in any of the scantily clad women who crowd the darkened, strobe lit room. In an instant and without hesitation, the stranger raises his assault rifle and steadies it at shoulder level. Gun-fire erupts. Mass hysteria follows. Hundreds of footsteps in every direction. Bodies crumpled. Limbs trampled. The smell of death lingers in the thick, sweat-filled air.

***

In the end, forty-two people lie dead, including the gunman, who died of a self-inflicted gunshot wound. This massacre stands as the worst mass shooting in the history of the state of New Jersey. The motive is still under investigation. Of the victims, all but two have been positively identified. These decedents, both female, were found to be in possession of counterfeit identification. Police have taken fingerprints and have collected DNA samples in an attempt to ascertain the identity of these individuals. Club Nitro remains closed pending further investigation.

BROTHERS BEFORE OTHERS

Hermosa Beach, California

The two strangers sit alone with each other in the living room, on opposite ends of the sofa. The man, Alan, is nervous. He struggles desperately to make small talk. The woman, Erin, is visibly annoyed. She appears impatient and cannot believe what she is hearing.

"So this genus is called Dorylus, otherwise known as the driver ant, and they're found primarily in Central and Eastern Africa. A friend of my father's brought them back for me on one of his business trips there, and I've had them since I was a kid. Anyway, I bet you didn't know that each colony can have over 20 million ants. Like most varieties, Dorylus ants are blind, and they communicate primarily through pheromones. How cool is that? It's sort of like a female ant wearing perfume to get the male ants' attention."

The awkward silence is deafening, broken only by the incessant, rhythmic thumping on the living room wall. This constant beat, intermixed with deep panting and high-pitched squealing, cannot be mistaken for anything but two lovers joined in ecstasy.

Oblivious to the obvious, Alan continues to drone on about the subculture of ants, but he is suddenly interrupted by his female counterpart.

"Are you for real? You're showing me some stupid-ass ant farm while those two are fucking their brains out in the next room. How can you even concentrate on anything right now?"

"I'm sorry. I guess I'm just used to it. I learned to tune out a lot of things living with Marcus. He has quite the reputation with the ladies."

The sexual sounds intensify and finally peak with an orgasmic crescendo worthy of an Academy Award.

"How the hell can you tune *that* out?"

"I don't know. I suppose I've had a lot of practice."

Rolling her eyes, Erin sits stoic with her arms folded across her bosom. Alan begins to perspire, and his mind races feverishly for something witty to say. He comes up with nothing. This quagmire seems to last an eternity. In actuality, it is no more than a few minutes. That is when the bedroom door opens, and out walks a beautiful young woman named Beverly. Her hair is matted and her makeup unkempt. Clearly, she is still enthralled by the cataclysmic sexual encounter she has just experienced.

"Are you ready to go, Erin?"

"Gee, Bev, I don't know. I was having so much fun here with Alex."

Alan corrects her.

"It's Alan."

Erin continues, "Looking at his bugs."

"They're ants," Alan remarks.

"I'm so glad we had the pleasure of meeting these two Casanovas at the club tonight. Plus, I got to listen to your head bounce off the bed board for the past hour. Why on earth would I want to leave?"

Entering from the bedroom, Marcus engages the trio.

"Yes, why *would* you want to leave?"

The silhouette of his shirtless form is highlighted by the room's recessed lighting. His oblique muscles are accentuated by faint beads of sweat. He stands six-foot-two and weighs 185 pounds, and he looks like he stepped straight out of the pages of GQ Magazine.

"How's it going, Alan? Did you and Erin get to know each other?"

"Not nearly as much as you and Beverly did," Alan says sheepishly.

"Oh, I had a great time here playing with Alex's bugs."

"They're ants. And it's Alan. My name is Alan."

"Whatever. Let's go, Bev."

Still in a post-sexual trance, Beverly kisses Marcus gently on the cheek and mouths the words "call me" as she walked to the door. Passing Alan, she cordially acknowledges him as she leaves.

"Good night, Alex."

The door slams shut.

"It's Alan. My name is Alan."

***

Alan Ackerman and Marcus Van Pelt have been friends for nearly ten years, having met during their freshman year at the University of Southern California, and are the epitome of the modern-day odd couple.

Alan is shy, introverted, and socially inept. He grew up an only child in a middle-class home in Glendale, California. His father, an electrical engineer, was a strict disciplinarian. His mother, a stay-at-home mom, kept him sheltered and isolated. He was home-schooled and often ostracized by other children in his neighborhood. Rarely did he make any friends. Considered a savant, Alan double majored in industrial engineering and entomology, which offered him the opportunity to pursue his true passions in life: molecular chemistry and insects.

In stark contrast, Marcus Van Pelt is a free-spirited extrovert who exudes confidence in just about any situation. He grew up traveling the country as a military brat. His father, a staff sergeant in the United States Army, met Marcus's mother, a Danish model, in the Netherlands during a military conference in the late 1980s. The two fell in love and traveled back to the States together. Although Marcus was conceived overseas, he was born on American soil. He holds the same dual citizenship as his mother, and prefers to use her family name, Van Pelt, for work purposes. Marcus's family settled in the Los Angeles County suburb of Calabasas, California. He attended the prestigious Calmont School, where many of his classmates were the children of celebrities. From an early age, he learned to use his good looks and charming personality to his advantage. After high school, he enrolled in the USC film school, where he studied drama. Yet to catch his big break, Marcus manages to land the occasional small role on television. Like most struggling actors, Marcus has to hustle to make ends meet. He supplements his income mainly by bartending and working as a personal trainer.

By chance, Marcus and Alan were paired up as lab partners in a chemistry class during their freshman year. Alan had taken the course as part of his required curriculum. Marcus, on the other hand, enrolled in it because he thought it would be a good place to meet shy, sexually curious women. These two divergent personalities came together and formed an unlikely yet unique bond. They are friends in the purest sense of the word. Friends who help each other. Friends who don't betray each other. No matter what. "Brothers before others" is a saying they frequently use to describe their commitment.

"That didn't go so well," remarks Alan.

"No, it didn't." Marcus says. "You showed her the ant farm, didn't you, Alan?"

"Yes. I showed her the ant farm."

"How many times have I told you, don't show them the ants?"

"A lot."

"Yes! A lot. No woman wants to see your ant collection."

"I know, but I thought this one was different. I thought she'd be interested in them."

"You thought she was *different*? Let me ask you a question. Does she have a vagina, Alan?"

"Well, as a matter of certainty, I couldn't tell you. But within a reasonable tolerance and statistical margin of error, I would have to say the answer to that question is yes."

"Okay then. Follow my logic here, buddy. I'm going to go slow for you so there won't be any misunderstanding. You ready?"

"Yes, I'm ready."

"Excellent. Here we go. If she has a vagina, Alan, then she is *not* different. She is the same as *every* other woman out there. They're *all* the same. And pussy is pussy. No matter how you slice it. Doesn't matter what color it is. What it looks like. What it tastes like. Pussy is pussy. You got it?"

"Yes, Marcus. I got it."

"Good. Now, for the last time, get rid of the damn ants!"

"You say that like it's so easy. They're like family to me. I've had this colony since I was thirteen years old. I've watched them grow and multiply, spawning new generations. They're smart. They're strong. They're like children to me. I've even named some of them."

"I'm sorry. Did you just say you named some of them? Jesus Christ, Alan. You need more help than I thought. Good thing I love you, pal. I'm going to jump in the shower and try to erase this conversation from my memory."

As Marcus leaves the room, Alan is left all alone. Alone with his thoughts. Alone with his ants. Alone.

The next morning, it is business as usual. Alan gets up and tends to his colony of ants. He then leaves for work at Cypress Laboratories, one of the leading developers of commercial-grade adhesives in the country. Alan is one of the engineers developing a new compound with an enhanced molecular base, in hopes of forming the perfect combination of strength, pliability, and flexibility.

Per his normal ritual, Marcus wakes and watches *Sports-Center* as he sips his protein shake and readies himself for his morning workout. Afterward, he stops at the homes of several clients for their weekly training sessions. At the end of the workday, Marcus and Alan meet at one of their favorite places, Rok Sushi Kitchen, for happy hour.

"What's going on, my man? How was work?"

"Actually, really good," replies Alan. "I made a huge breakthrough."

"Oh yeah? Sweet. Tell me you finally talked to that college intern, you dog."

"Well, not exactly. I was referring to a breakthrough I made with EC-2250X."

"Uh, okay. But you lost me with 'not exactly.' What the hell are you talking about?"

"EC-2250X. It's that new super-adhesive I told you about awhile back."

"Oh yeah. How exhilarating. How could I possibly forget?"

"Your sarcasm is duly noted, Marcus. So moving on, we performed strength and tolerance testing today. And guess what."

"You accidentally glued your nut sack to your inner thigh."

"Close. Do you care to take another guess."

"Do tell, Alan. The suspense is killing me."

"Well, it blew past our wildest expectations. Here's how it goes. Epoxy testing is done in two separate categories: lap shear strength and compressive strength. Lap shear determines the overall strength of an epoxy and also its mode of failure. Compressive measures the ability for the epoxy to handle weight."

"Wow, Alan. All this sexy talk about epoxies is getting me hard."

"I'm serious, man. This is huge. Now, both of these are measured in units of psi. That stands for pounds per square inch."

"No shit. I know what psi stands for, dude."

"Okay, sorry. Now get this. The lap shear strength of an ordinary epoxy is 2500 psi. The average compressive strength is about 10,000 psi. EC-2250X recorded a lap shear strength of 10,000 psi and a compressive strength of 40,000 psi. That's four times the strength of the most powerful epoxy currently on the market. Four times!"

"Alan, I can also do basic arithmetic. It was a struggle, but I did manage to pass the third grade. Look, man. I'm happy your tests went well. I'm just disappointed. Like I said before, I was hoping you were going to tell me you finally talked to that intern or something like that. What's your hesitation?"

"I don't know, Marcus. I'm just not like you in that regard. I don't have your body *or* your good looks."

"No, you don't. But you can have my confidence. All you have to do is try. I've told you that over and over again. Smile at them, Alan. Say hello to them, Alan. Talk to them, Alan. Take interest in them, Alan. But no. You don't do any of that. I'm trying to help you here, brother. I'm trying to get you over your fears so you can finally score with the ladies. But it's almost like you don't even give a shit. I mean, look around you. Look at all this ass just waiting to be tapped. Come on, man. It's like shooting fish in a barrel."

Marcus stops talking and looks up to see Alan sulking and totally dejected. Realizing he might have been a little hard on him, Marcus eases up a bit.

"Listen, man, I'm sorry for coming down on you. I just want you to meet somebody special and be happy. That's all."

"It's all right, Marcus. I know you're looking out for me. I guess I just have to be more open-minded and try harder."

"You'll be fine, bro. Trust me. I wouldn't steer you wrong. You're my boy, Alan. A little mentally unstable, but still my boy."

"Thanks, Marcus. Brothers before others?"

"Abso-fucking-lutely! Now, let's get a drink and see how we do tonight."

As is customary, Marcus is making time with various women throughout the evening. After he courts one sultry vixen in particular, while at the same time making certain she has an available friend for Alan to entertain, the foursome leave Rok Sushi and head to the men's apartment for a nightcap.

The evening abruptly comes to an end after Alan introduces his guest to his prized ants. In his defense, he could not have possibly known the girl suffers from myrmecophobia, the inexplicable fear of ants. Terrified and in a full-blown panic attack, she bursts into Marcus's bedroom in hysterics. His partner quickly reaches for her clothing and, while still half-dressed, is literally pulled out of the apartment by her delirious friend, leaving the two men alone with each other.

"I'm going to make this short and sweet. Alan, I love you like a brother. But this shit has got to stop. I'm out of patience. Lose the ants! Now, if you'll excuse me, I'm going to take what's left of my hard-on and try to rub one out so I can fall asleep and forget this nightmare ever happened. Good night."

As he's left alone once again, a tear begins to stream down Alan's cheek. As he looks at his beloved ants, he cannot fathom parting ways with them. Yet he knows Marcus is right. Something has to give.

The next day, Marcus is training one of his long-standing clients, who also happens to be his former lover, Desiree Morgan, when he suddenly gets an idea.

"I'm telling you, Desiree. The guy just needs a little push to boost his confidence. You should go out with him. Make him feel good about himself. Show some interest. He needs that right now."

"Marcus, honey, you know I would do anything for you. But isn't your roommate a little weird? I mean, what's with the ants in his room? That's really creepy."

"Don't get me started. I'm working on that. And yes. He has his quirks. But he's a solid guy. I'm telling you. He just needs some confidence. A little push. Please, Des. Go out with him this one time. That's all I ask. What's the worst that can happen?"

"I can't believe I'm going to say *yes* to this."

"You'll do it? Thank you! Thank you so much, Des. I owe you big time. All right, here's how we'll set it up, because it has to look like a chance meeting. He eats lunch every day at this place called Bernie's..."

***

The following Monday, Alan finds himself waiting in line to order his usual lunch at Bernie's Café. Momentarily preoccupied, he doesn't even notice the stunning redhead standing behind him in line. The temptress only gets Alan's attention when she orders the exact same lunch: tuna on rye, a cup of vegetable soup, and an iced tea.

"That sounds really good. I think I'll have the same."

Instead of taking the opening cue, Alan stutters and fumbles for the right words. Sensing his nervousness, Desiree takes over and extends her hand.

"Hi. I'm Desiree."

Quick to return her gesture, Alan lurches forward and knocks over his soup while reaching for Desiree's hand. Her dress and shoes are now covered in beef broth and vegetables. Alan does the only thing any self-respecting man in his position could do: he grovels for forgiveness.

"Oh my God. I'm so sorry. I'm such an idiot. I'll pay for your dry cleaning. I promise. Are you okay?"

To her credit, Desiree keeps her composure and remembers the words Marcus told her.

"It's all right. These things happen. I've been meaning to go shopping for some new outfits anyway."

Her sense of humor is disarming and puts Alan at ease. He starts to relax and feels calm around her. Remembering Marcus's pep-talk, Alan actually musters the courage to ask her out on a date. When she accepts his offer, he can't help but think how proud Marcus will be when he hears the good news.

After work, Alan rushes home and excitedly bursts into conversation about his midday encounter with the mysterious female.

"Marcus, I'm so glad you're home!"

"What's up, Big Al?"

"I just wanted to apologize for the other day. I guess I'm just overly sensitive about things. I know you only want to help me get over my fears. And with that said, I'll have you know today I met a woman."

"No shit! That's great."

"Her name's Desiree, and I ran into her at Bernie's during my lunch break. Actually, to be technical, I spilled soup on her. But that doesn't matter now."

"Wait. What? You spilled soup on her?"

"Forget about that. The important thing is I asked her out on a date. A real date. Not the kind you have to pay for either. And get this. She actually said *yes*. What do you think of that?"

"I think that's awesome, bro. I knew you had it in you. I'm happy for you, Alan. You see? I told you a little confidence goes a long way."

"You're right, Marcus. You're always right when it comes to this topic. You're a true friend. You really are."

Marcus just smiles and acknowledges the compliment. However, he can't help but think Alan would be crushed if he knew the truth. He doesn't particularly like being deceptive with his friend. But it's for his own good. *Besides,* he thinks to himself, *what's the worst that could happen? It's one harmless date. It's not as if Alan is going to fall in love or anything.*

***

Two weeks have passed since their initial encounter. During that time, Alan and Desiree shared several phone calls. After each conversation, Alan finds himself falling harder and harder for her. She makes him feel safe enough to be himself and let his guard down. Alan is experiencing a connection he has never felt in the past. In fact, he is already in love.

On the night of their rendezvous, Alan picks her up at her home then drives straight to his apartment, insisting that Marcus meet the woman of his dreams.

"Desiree, this is my roommate, Marcus. He's my best friend in the whole world. And Marcus, this is Desiree, the amazing woman I told you about."

The cohorts lock eyes and exchange smirks as Marcus offers his hand in an exercise of cordiality.

"Hello, Desiree. It's nice to *finally* meet you."

"Likewise. It's a pleasure."

The two engage in small talk for several minutes until Alan abruptly interrupts.

"I want to give you something, Desiree. Now, close your eyes, because it's a surprise."

Understandably apprehensive, Desiree does as she's told, as Alan continues, "Now, hold out your hand, and keep those eyes closed."

Alan places a small, folded cloth into her outstretched hand.

"Open your eyes."

He then unwraps it and reveals the contents, a sterling silver pendant attached to a matching linked chain. Based on the stellar old-world craftsmanship and ornate detail, it is clear the piece is vintage. The front of the oblong medallion boasts a setting sun. The back is engraved with the Hebrew inscription "ATA KOL KAKH KHASHUV LI," which translates to, "YOU MEAN SO MUCH TO ME."

"My grandfather gave this necklace to my grandmother while they were still living in Eastern Europe. They weren't even married yet. In fact, he had just met her several weeks earlier. But he knew they were destined to be together; that's why he gave it to her. And she knew it too; that's why she accepted it. Even when they were separated into different concentration camps, they never lost faith they would one day be together again. Somehow, my grandmother managed to keep it hidden from the Nazis the entire time. In 1945, when Europe was finally liberated at the end of the war, my grandparents were among the survivors. They were the lucky ones. They used to tell people their love and devotion to each other kept them alive. They had to survive for each other. Shortly after being reunited, they married and left for America, with my grandmother wearing this very pendant around her neck. When she passed, she left it to me because I was the sole grandchild responsible for carrying on our family name. Now, I'm giving it to you."

In stunned disbelief, Desiree is at a loss for words, but she finally begins, "Alan, there is no way I can accept this from you. It's too much."

"Nonsense," Alan states as he places the necklace around her neck. "It's perfect for you. And we are perfect together. Now, let's go. We don't want to be late. Dinner reservations are for 8 p.m. sharp."

Alan hurries a still-baffled Desiree out the door and addresses the man responsible for his newly found confidence and good fortune.

"Have a great night, Marcus. And don't bother waiting up."

As the door slams shut, Marcus stares blankly at the wall. He can't believe what he just witnessed. He thinks, *I don't think this is going to end well.*

Later that evening, when Alan returns home, he finds Marcus sitting alone in the living room.

"Hey, Marcus. I thought I told you not to wait up."

"I couldn't sleep. I have a lot on my mind."

"What's the matter? Is it work?"

"No, Alan. It *isn't* work."

"What is it then?"

"It's you, Alan! All right, I'm concerned about you! Don't you think you came on a little strong tonight?"

"What are you talking about?"

"What am I talking about? I don't know. How about we start with the fact you gave a perfect stranger your dead grandmother's necklace she smuggled back from the Holocaust. How's that for starters?"

"How dare you! Desiree is not a stranger! She's the love of my life!"

"Good God Almighty! You don't even know her, Alan. How could you say you love her? You know nothing about her."

"I know enough to know what I feel is real. And she feels it too. Besides, *you* were the one who told me to take a chance. To be confident. To act instead of react. I finally did all those things and found someone to care about, who also cares about me. And *now* you want to dissuade me from my happiness?"

"No, I want to dissuade you from getting hurt, Alan. Can't you see that? This is heading for disaster. This wasn't supposed to be..."

Marcus suddenly stops mid-sentence so as not to reveal the truth behind his relationship with Desiree and his involvement with Alan's meeting her.

Always astute, Alan picks up on the verbal faux pas and probes the issue.

"What's that supposed to mean?"

"Nothing, man. Just forget it."

"Oh, I get it now. It just became crystal clear to me. You're jealous."

"Jealous? Is that what you think?"

"Of course. You meant to say *I* wasn't the one who was supposed to find true love. It was supposed to be you. You can't stand the fact I'm finally happy, and you're not. All those one-night stands are meaningless. They don't count for shit. They can't compare with true love."

"You're living in a fucking fantasy land, bro. You are so far removed from reality right now, I can't even. I'm done. Good night, jackass."

"I love you too, Marcus. Asshole."

***

The next day, Marcus reaches out to Desiree and invites her over to discuss the current situation in hopes of rectifying it. She agrees to meet him and arrives at the apartment just before noon.

Marcus begins, "What in the holy hell happened last night?"

"Oh, you know. Nothing special. Just a typical first date where the overtly sheltered and clinically disturbed guy decides to give the extremely good-natured and fun-loving girl his dead grandmother's irreplaceable necklace. That's all. What the hell did you get me into?"

"I know. Things got a little out of hand."

"A *little* out of hand? That's a fucking understatement if I've ever heard one. 'He needs some confidence. He just needs a little push. Just go out with him one time. What's the worst that can happen?' That's what you said to me, Marcus. You never told me he was this desperate."

"All right, calm down, doll."

"Do *not* tell me to calm down. No woman likes to be told to calm down. You of all people should know that."

"Point taken, Des. I get it. Listen, tell him you just got out of a long-term relationship and that you're not looking for anything serious right now. And leave it at that."

"Yeah, right. You think it's going to be that easy? The guy thinks we're soul mates for Chrissake. I mean, you should have seen the way he was staring at me all night. I felt like a bird in a cage. It was so freaking creepy. All he kept talking about was how fate brought us together, and how he waited his whole life to meet someone like me. It was nauseating."

"I can only imagine. Oh, and make sure you give him back the necklace."

"Obviously. You think I want to keep this God-awful thing? The only reason I'm still wearing it is I'm afraid he's following me."

"Trust me, Des. He's not following you. Alan is a total creature of habit. I guarantee he's at work right now eating the same lunch he spilled on you the other day."

"I'm glad you can make jokes and laugh right now, but this isn't funny. I never should've let you talk me into this."

"I'm sorry, Des. I'm just trying to lighten up the mood."

"Yeah, well, when I get this worked up, I need to get my frustrations out in a bad way. What do you do to get your frustrations out, Marcus?"

With that loaded question, Marcus and Desiree aren't able to resist their primal urges any longer. They lunge toward each other and embrace. Lips join. Tongues tangle. On instinct, they make their way to Marcus's bedroom, pawing animalistically at each other's clothing, leaving a littered trail of garments in their wake.

Amid this orgiastic feast of passion, an unmindful Alan enters the apartment. As always, Alan's conscience has gotten the better of him. The fight he had with Marcus troubles him. What's more, he's mad at himself for saying those awful things to his best and only friend – so much so that Alan deviates from his normal routine and decides to come home during his lunch hour to apologize.

After stepping into the living room, seeing the scattered clothing and smelling the pungent scent of sex in the air, Alan realizes Marcus is preoccupied. He quietly turns and tries not to be noticed while making his exit. However, he is distracted by a glimpse of afternoon sunlight that pierces his eye. This beam reflects off a shiny metallic object, which is embedded in the thick, fibrous carpeting.

Alan bends down to retrieve the rogue item but immediately regrets his decision. Time stands still. His eyes become transfixed on the words that are forever etched into his brain: "ATA KOL KAKH KHASHUV LI."

Alan's temporary trance is broken by an all-too-familiar sound coming from Marcus's bedroom.

"Oh God, Marcus. Yes! Fuck me harder! Fuck me harder! Ohhhhh!"

"Is that what you want, Des? You dirty little girl."

"Oh yes! Yes! Yes! I'm going to cum, baby. Oh my God! Oh fuck, yeah!"

Unable to move, Alan listens as Marcus and Desiree climax simultaneously.

"There, Marcus. Now, don't you feel better?"

"Hell yeah. It's been so long since we've been together I almost forgot what it was like to fuck you."

"Who are you kidding? You could never forget me."

"True that. Poor Alan doesn't know what he's missing."

"Stop. Don't ruin the moment by bringing him up. I'm still freaked out by all this."

"Fair enough. I'm sure Alan is going to call you later. When he does, tell him what we talked about. I tried talking to him yesterday, but he ripped me a new asshole when I said he was rushing into things with you."

As if injected with a shot of adrenaline, Alan regains his wits and bolts stealth-like out of the apartment just as Marcus and Desiree emerge from the confines of the bedroom.

Later that evening, Alan returns home from the lab and finds his roommate reading over a script for an upcoming audition.

"Hey, Alan. How was work, buddy?

At first, Alan ignores the greeting and is preoccupied with a package he's carrying.

"Alan? You there?"

"Yes. I'm here, Marcus."

"You okay, man? You seem a little off."

"Yeah. I'm good. Just have a lot on my plate right now. Desiree called me. She said she wanted to talk. I told her it was best if she met me here."

"Desiree is coming *here*?"

"Yes. I insisted. Is that okay?"

"Oh sure, man. Of course it's okay. I just thought she was gonna...never mind. It's cool. I'll head out and give you your privacy."

"No! I want you to stay. I think you were right. I came on way too strong. It's too soon. And I don't really know her all that well. I think she's going to break things off with me. I need you here for support. After all, you're my best friend."

"Sure, man. I'll be here for you. Brothers before others, right?"

Alan nods in agreement.

A short time later, Desiree arrives at the apartment and is greeted at the door by Alan, who is in an extraordinarily good mood.

"Hello, my sweet. Come on in. You remember my roommate, Marcus, don't you?"

"Yes, of course I do. Hello, Marcus."

"Hi, Desiree. Long time no see," says Marcus with a coy smile.

Alan continues, "Thanks for coming over to talk. But before you begin, I already know what you're going to say."

"You do?"

"Yes, I do. Clearly, you're not ready for a relationship of this magnitude. You're not looking for the same things I am. You also think I was too forward and found it strange I entrusted you with a priceless family keepsake so rich in history and so very close to my heart. Speaking of which, may I?"

Desiree breathes a sigh of relief as Alan reaches behind her neck and unclasps his grandmother's necklace. Gripping it tight, he continues, "I'm sorry that things didn't exactly work out for us the way I wanted. But I am grateful for our chance meeting. It made me reevaluate some things in my life. I realize relationships and friendships are of the utmost importance. The cornerstone of both is trust. Without trust, we simply cannot survive. Take Marcus and me. We've been friends for ten years now. Our bond is stronger than ever. We don't keep secrets or lie to each other. We're honest in our thoughts and opinions, even if we don't always agree on things. We always help each other in times of need. Isn't that right, buddy?"

"Absolutely, Alan. We're friends 'till the end."

"Well, Desiree, I hope when you're finally ready to settle down, you find someone as trustworthy as Marcus because he's the type of man who would treat you like a princess. Just like I would have done. You know, it's a shame the two of you didn't meet by chance. You make a great-looking couple."

Not sure what to make of Alan's last comment, Marcus and Desiree remain silent.

Alan speaks up once more and pours a celebratory drink to share with them.

"A toast to eternal friendships, everlasting love, and unwavering trust."

Following Alan's lead, Marcus and Desiree join in and raise their glasses in an impromptu show of solidarity with Alan after his prophetic salute.

***

Early the next morning, a groggy Marcus Van Pelt attempts to open his eyes. He is nauseated and has blurred vision. He attempts to move but finds himself in a quasi-paralytic state. Totally disoriented, he begins to blink rapidly in hopes of sharpening his vision. With his anxiety heightened, he attempts to raise his arms. He cannot. He tries to bend his knees but fails. With all of his might, he struggles to arch his back and push himself up but fails once again.

Panic-stricken, Marcus desperately needs help. However, he finds himself all alone. Nonetheless, he musters up the strength and screams for the person who has always been there for him.

"Alan!"

His cries for help are answered immediately.

"Why are you yelling, Marcus? I'm right here next to you."

Unable to move his head, Marcus shifts his gaze in the direction of Alan's voice. Seeing him struggle, Alan takes a step to the side and aligns himself directly with Marcus's field of vision. He then repeats himself in a whisper.

"I'm right here."

"What the fuck is going on? What is this? Where the hell am I?"

"Of your three questions, Marcus, the last one puzzles me. How could you *not* know where you are? You've spent so much time here. It's your favorite place – the room you frequent most often. You're in your own bedroom, Marcus. And we're all here with you."

His mind and heart race. His senses on high alert. Marcus frantically tries to comprehend Alan's words.

"What do you mean, *we*? Who's *we*?

"You, me, and Desiree, of course."

Marcus bellows in sheer terror.

"Nooooo!"

Marcus and Desiree are both nude, their bodies conjoined together. His bed serves as the canvas for this art exhibition.

"I'm surprised she hasn't woken up yet. I thought I calculated the dosage of Rohypnol properly. I'm sorry, buddy. I guess I got a little sloppy in my haste."

"You sick fuck! What did you do?"

"Whoa. Easy, Marcus. You're being a bit hostile. I really don't like your tone. I mean, after all, I've taken the trouble to *reconnect* you with one of your former lovers. No pun intended. I thought you'd be more appreciative."

"Now, to answer your question as to what I did. I simply took it upon myself to continue my research testing on EC-2250X. You do remember me telling you about that, correct? Just in case it slipped your mind, let me refresh your memory. EC-2250X is the super adhesive I've helped create. We're at the stage where our legal team has to draft the warning labels for packaging. I figured I would help them out a little bit. And after seeing this result, I think it's safe to say the phrase "Avoid direct contact with skin" should most definitely be included. What do you think, Marcus? We can never be too careful. Extra precaution is always prudent. I mean, I would hate to see anyone get *stuck* in a precarious situation because of our negligence. Hehe. This time, the pun was intended."

"But why, Alan? Why? I...I tried to help you. Why?"

"You did help me, Marcus. In more ways than you realize. You liberated me. You gave me the confidence to be my own person and to confront any situation. You taught me not to be afraid of change. That it's okay to deviate from my normal routine. Thanks to you, I'm now able to do things in life that I never would have dreamed of in the past. I'm now able to let go of certain things in my life

I was holding onto out of fear. Fear of losing my identity. Fear of the unknown. But I'm not afraid anymore. And I owe it all to you. The only regret I have is I didn't listen to you sooner. I should have taken your advice long ago. Things probably would have been different today if I had. But, like they say, better late than never. I'm finally ready to move on. You'll be happy to know, Marcus, that I've decided, with your help of course, it's time to get rid of the ants."

At this time, Alan reaches down and picks up an enormous plastic storage container, which houses his entire colony of driver ants – all 20 million of them. They're smart. They're strong. They're Alan's children. And they're extremely hungry.

"You know, over the past couple of weeks, I've been so preoccupied with Desiree here, I'm ashamed to say I've neglected my children. I haven't talked to them. I haven't played with them. And what's worse, I haven't even fed them. Speaking of eating, did you know a fully mature colony of driver ants is capable of devouring an entire Cape buffalo? That's nearly 1,500 pounds. It's been documented in the wild. The only parts left behind are bone and horns. Well, technically, a horn is a permanent pointed projection that consists of a covering of keratin and other proteins that surround a core of live bone. So I suppose one could make the argument that bone and horn could be synonymous. Would you listen to me? I'm sorry, Marcus. I'm digressing. Where are my manners? Let me get back on topic. Like I was saying, you've helped me so much I could never really repay you. And now, you're going to help my children too. You're going to help them survive. Help them spawn new generations. You're going to serve as the food source they so desperately need."

Amid the shrieks of terror, Alan stands over his victims with a devious smile and releases his children. In an instant, the colony engulfs Marcus and Desiree, turning them into a human smorgasbord. Every orifice, every crack, and every crevice is inundated by the insatiable hungry swarm.

Perhaps it is the sensation of 20 million carnivorous ants stimulating her nerve endings. Or Alan's rudimentary medicinal cocktail has finally run its course and worn off. Either way, Desiree regains consciousness just long enough to hear Alan's chilling voice echoing in her ears, as he revels in his new-found power.

"I was right. The two of you do make a great-looking couple. But take my advice. Don't rush into things. You should take it slow. Get to know each other. The last thing you want is to be *stuck* with someone you really have nothing in common with. Ahahaha! Again, with the puns. I can't help it. I crack myself up."

Alan marvels at the sight in front of him. He relishes in their coughing and choking as their throats are filled by the ant parade. Their bodies convulse. Their exposed flesh is red with legions, puss-filled, and blistered. What is left of their muffled screams is furthered stifled when Alan turns on his iPod. He programmed the device to play a continuous loop of his favorite childhood song.

"The ants go marching one by one. Hoorah! Hoorah! The ants go marching one by one. Hoorah! Hoorah! The ants go marching one by one. The little one stops to suck his thumb. And they all go marching down to the ground. To get out of the rain. BOOM! BOOM! BOOM! BOOM! BOOM! BOOM! BOOM! BOOM!"

As he steps out of the apartment for the last time and locks the door behind him, Alan unabashedly begins his new life in a world full of fresh possibilities. A world without his cherished ants. A world without his best friend, Marcus. A world without his beloved Desiree. For the first time in his life, Alan Ackerman is on his own. He is free. Free to travel wherever the road takes him.

"The ants go marching two by two. Hoorah! Hoorah! The ants go marching two by two Hoorah! Hoorah! The ants go marching two by two. The little one stops to tie his shoe. And they all go marching down to the ground. To get out of the rain. BOOM! BOOM! BOOM! BOOM! BOOM! BOOM! BOOM! BOOM!"

LAST CALL

It's an unseasonably warm night for late November. For Harry Wozniak, it seems like he's been walking for hours. In reality, Harry lost all concept of time the moment he opened his bedroom door and discovered his wife, Julie, in bed with their neighbor, Dominick. For months, Harry had suspected something was out of the norm. On more than one occasion, he voiced his concerns to Julie. However, like a true master-manipulator, she deflected blame and re-directed it at Harry. She mocked him and said he was being ridiculous.

"He's our next-door neighbor, Harry. We're only friends. Stop being so damn paranoid. You're embarrassing yourself."

Despite her assurances to the contrary, Harry still couldn't shake the feeling something just wasn't right. On this particular afternoon, something prompted him to stop home mid-shift, something he had never done in the past fifteen years working at the electrical plant. As he walked in the back door and made his way toward the master bedroom, his head told him to turn around and go back to work. However, his heart had to know the truth.

Julie and Dominick were oblivious to Harry's presence. They were too enthralled with each other to even realize he hovered over them. Harry watched as the love of his life climaxed with another man, in a fit of furious passion that he himself had never brought her to achieve. Without saying a word, Harry removed the .357 Magnum snub-nosed revolver from his waistband. He raised and leveled the gun to the back of Julie's head and squeezed the trigger. With Dominick still inside her, Harry pumped a second shot into her lifeless body. He then turned his attention to his neighbor, a so-called friend, whose face and upper torso were already adorned with a copious amount of blood and brain matter. The first shot struck Dominick square between the eyes, killing him instantly. In a moment of poetic justice, Harry placed a second round directly into the dead man's scrotum.

For the past several hours, Harry has been aimlessly roaming the streets, his head cluttered with a million and one thoughts.

It was a crime of passion. No jury would convict me. They have to believe me. Anybody else in my situation would have done the same exact thing.

Continuing his journey, Harry finds himself in one of the seediest areas of Trenton, New Jersey. Although less than ten miles from his delicate, suburban neighborhood of Hamilton, Harry is a world away from home. He stops at the corner of Ewing Street and Ogden Avenue. The tavern called Willie's Place is a hole in the wall. Nonetheless, it's exactly what Harry needs. Cheap booze and a place to rest. No one will recognize him here. He'll have time to think and figure out what to do next.

Opening the door, he enters the dimly lit, smoke-filled room. Harry tries not to make direct eye contact with anyone as he surveys the crowd. It's quite a colorful cast of characters. Two young, Latino males are shooting pool. There's a hooker standing in the corner near the men's room, most likely where she does most of her business. Several other sketchy looking patrons loiter around the bar, nursing strong drinks and keeping to themselves. Harry pulls up a seat, where he is greeted by the bartender.

"What'll it be, friend?"

The man is gruff and weathered. He rests his meaty hands flat on the counter and leans in to offer Harry a light for his smoke.

"Thanks, pal. Just give me a shot of Jack and back it up with a Bud."

"You got it."

Harry sizes him up. It's clear he's been around the block a few times. No doubt he's got some skeletons of his own. To work in a place like this, you'd have to be running from something.

"Here you go. Salute."

With a nod of his head, Harry slams the Jack and chases it with a swig of beer.

"Keep 'em coming," he says, as he taps his fingers on the bar top.

After throwing back six of Lynchburg's finest soldiers, plus another four beers in tow, Harry is feeling no pain. Despite being three sheets to the wind, his recollection of the day's events remains lucid. He keeps replaying the scene over and over in his head.

I didn't do anything wrong. The bitch cheated on me with my neighbor. What was I supposed to do?

His conscience is starting to get the best of him. If he doesn't talk to somebody soon, he's going to break down completely.

What are bartenders for, if not to listen to people's problems? He'll understand. He has to. He's not doing anything else anyway. He has to hear me out.

Harry begins, "So, you been here a long time, huh?"

"Longer than you can imagine."

"Hmm. I bet. Anyway, uh, I'm sure you've seen *and* heard your share of fucked up things."

"Oh yeah."

"I mean, people must tell you all sorts of crazy shit, right?"

"I've heard it all, my friend. I've heard it all."

"Well, I need to lay something on you then."

Waving a dismissive hand, the bartender interrupts.

"Let me stop you right there. There's no need."

"Yes, there is. I need to get this off my chest."

"No, you don't understand. What I mean is, there's no need for you to feel guilty. They both got what they deserved, Harry."

A cold chill runs down Harry's spine, as a look of bewilderment etches across his face.

"What the fuck? You...you called me 'Harry.'"

"Yes, of course I did. That's your name."

"How do you know that? Who the hell are you? And what do you mean, 'They got what they deserved'?"

"I'm talking about Julie and Dominick. They totally got what they deserved."

The barstool crashes to the ground as Harry jumps to his feet. He backs up and places some distance between himself and the stranger. In a panic, he pulls out his gun and points it at his mysterious nemesis.

Harry demands, "You're going to tell me right now who you are and how you know all this, or I swear to God, I'll kill you right on the spot."

Calmly, the man offers his retort.

"No you won't, Harry. You're out of bullets."

"Like hell I am. This is a five-shot Smith. I only used four rounds. Each of the bastards got two apiece. That means I still have one in the pipe. And I'm about to use it if you don't tell me what the hell is going on!"

"I'm telling you the truth, Harry. I wouldn't lie to you. The gun is empty. If you don't believe me, just crack open the cylinder and see for yourself."

With a trembling hand, Harry fumbles with the cylinder release and pops it open. Not daring to take his eyes off the man, he cants the gun and empties the contents into the palm of his hand. He ever so slightly shifts his focus downward and incredulously gawks at a fist full of empty shell casings, five to be exact.

"But...but I shot each of them twice. Two...two times each. I'm certain of it. What happened to the last bullet?"

The man remains silent. His cool, steel gaze pierces Harry's eyes as if casting a spell.

With much trepidation, Harry reaches up and grabs the back of his head. His hand is immediately enveloped in a wet, fleshy crater. Pulling his hand away, Harry watches as the crimson-colored paste seeps through his fingertips onto the floor below.

"Look around you, Harry. This time, take a *good* look and tell me what you see."

Harry looks at the men near the pool table. He notices they both appear to be bleeding from their chest.

"Are those gunshot wounds?"

"That's right, Harry. Those two guys were shot and killed by the police earlier today during a botched robbery at a Wawa."

Next, Harry turns toward the hooker. She has heavy bruises on her face and a gaping wound to her neck.

"What happened to her?"

"Funny you should ask. This poor girl had a bad habit of coming up short with her payments to her pimp. The first time it happened, he gave her a beating as a warning. The next time, he slit her throat."

"What about that guy over there? What the hell happened to his head? Half of it is missing."

"You mean the black guy sitting at the high-top table? He's a gang banger who got caught walking through a rival's territory. A shotgun blast to his skull settled that dispute."

"This isn't real."

"Not real?" pulling down his own collar, "Are these real, Harry?"

The ligature marks on the man's throat run deep.

"Go ahead and place your fingers in the indentation. You should be able to feel my crushed windpipe."

"Fuck that."

"You shouldn't be surprised. A guy can only endure working in a place like this for so long. I had enough. So yesterday I decided to hang myself in the basement, right after we closed for the night."

"This...this can't be happening."

"It's already happened, Harry. Come on, I want to show you something."

"No way. I'm not going anywhere with you. You're a fucking liar. This is just a dream, a bad fucking dream. I'm out of here."

Harry pulls on the handle and yanks open the door. He finds himself on a threshold, caught between two very distinct places. As he stands in the doorway looking outside, the urban setting has vanished. It has been replaced by the inside of a home. Specifically, the image of a bedroom is staring back at him. It is a gruesome crime scene, one of a double-murder-suicide.

Two lovers, intertwined with each other, lie naked on the bed. A river of blood rages unchecked between them. The third corpse lies on the floor at the foot of the bed. It is the body of a man, still clutching the murder weapon, a stainless-steel, two-inch barrel, .357 Magnum revolver. The smell of gunpowder lingers in the air as blood flows freely from the gaping exit wound in the back of his head.

"It can't be," says Harry.

"I'm sorry, my friend. But unfortunately, it's time to go."

"But I don't understand. Go where?"

"It's last call."

DADDY'S LITTLE GIRL

"Daddy, it hurts."

"I know, sweetheart. Daddy's here. Try to think about something else."

"I can't. It really hurts."

Kevin McAdams is a single father. His wife was killed in a car crash last year. His eight-year-old daughter, Katie, suffers from the same childhood disease that ravaged his body thirty years earlier. The congenital abnormality, called polycystic kidney disease, is hereditary. Katie is currently in kidney failure and is in dire need of a transplant. She lost one of her kidneys three years ago. Her remaining one is slowly dying...and so is she.

"Daddy, it hurts. Make it stop, Daddy. Make it stop."

"I know it hurts, baby girl. I know. I'll find a way to make it stop. I promise."

Kevin desperately tries to console his daughter, but his hopes are bleak.

How many empty promises can I make? How many times can I tell her everything will be okay?

Her questions strike hard and weigh heavy. Yet he has no answers.

"Daddy, why am I always so sick? I don't want to stay in the hospital anymore."

"You have to be here for now, baby. The doctors are all working very hard to make you feel better."

"Why did God take Mommy away from us? I want Mommy."

Her words pierce the veil of his soul, leaving him naked and vulnerable.

Fuck. I feel so helpless.

His thoughts drift back to his childhood, a time spent in and out of hospitals dealing with a host of medical issues. At the age of sixteen, while recuperating from the surgery that removed his own kidney, Kevin committed himself at that very moment to helping others. He went on to medical school and ultimately became a pediatric surgeon.

Despite being a pioneer at the forefront of numerous medical innovations, Kevin cannot escape the irony that serves as a cerebral parasite. Over time, it has festered and grown stronger. To this day, it continues to devour his psyche. Regardless of his remarkable ability to breathe new life into countless children, he remains powerless to save his own flesh and blood.

This, however, is not the only cross that Kevin bears. There is another burdensome reality that is equally as crippling. After his wife's accident, Kevin didn't harvest her organs as a practical precaution. He can never forgive himself for such an error in judgment.

Why, God, why? Why didn't I see this coming? How could I have been so stupid? I should've had the foresight. Madeline could have given our little girl the gift of life for a second time. I'm sorry, my love. I failed you. I failed Katie. Please forgive me.

But there is no time to weep. Kevin has a job to do. His daughter needs him now more than ever.

"I'm tired, Daddy. I want to go to sleep."

Sensing the end could come swiftly amid a deep sleep, Kevin pleads with Katie to resist the urge.

"Don't go to sleep, baby. Stay up with Daddy. Let's play a game."

Katie has been on the waiting list for a kidney for nearly nine months. Each time a potential donor surfaces, the end result is always the same. Incorrect blood type, too low a level of blood antibodies, incompatible tissue match. Whatever the reason, Katie has been passed over each and every time.

As a man of medicine, Kevin is all too familiar with what lies ahead. His daughter grows weaker by the day. Her spirits are low. Her will to survive dwindles before his beleaguered eyes. He frantically struggles for a solution.

Think, damn it. There has to be a way.

"I miss Mommy. I want to see her again."

Katie fades in and out of consciousness. The unfiltered toxins course freely through her veins, attacking what few healthy cells remain.

Maybe the other doctors are right. Maybe I should just make her comfortable and let God's will be done.

Like so many others who have been forced to confront the eternal question of mortality, Kevin has systematically worked his way through the five stages of grief. His adamant denial. His fierce anger. His hopeful bargaining. His deep depression. All of these emotions have led him to the point of acceptance. He now realizes there is only one thing left to do. Kevin stares intently at his hands. Hands that are steady. Hands that are strong. Hands that are capable. Hands that have saved lives. Hands that will perform one more miracle.

The cold steel blade pierces the skin and glides effortlessly through layers of tendons and muscle. Thick sinew offers little resistance compared with the graceful maneuvering of this skilled surgeon. His arm, firmly encased within the abdominal cavity, feels warm and moist. The massive adrenalin overload fuels his blind instinct as he fishes his way until reaching the target. With the bean shaped organ firmly in his grasp, Kevin literally holds Katie's life in the palm of his hand.

A moment later, the adrenalin dump takes over, propelling Kevin's body into a state of shock. He collapses in a heap at the foot of his daughter's bed, covered in blood, still clutching his own kidney. As his world fades to black, Kevin looks up at Katie, who is smiling upon him.

"I told you I'd find a way to make it all better, baby girl."

"Thank you, Daddy. I always knew you would. But can we go see Mommy now? I'm ready, and she's been waiting for us for so long."

Kevin returns the smile. He reaches up and takes hold of Katie's hand.

"Yes, sweetie. I'm ready too. I love you so much. Let's go see Mommy together, as a family."

A GAMER'S ODYSSEY

"There's nowhere for you to hide, Izzy," a confident Michael Weslock boasts.

Michael is a sixteen-year-old junior at Jefferson High School in Rockford, Illinois. He lives in a modest home with his parents and his twelve-year-old sister, Abby. Michael – or Wes, as his circle of gaming cohorts refer to him – is currently enthralled in one of his favorite video games, *Urban Warrior*. Only he and his virtual pal, Izzy, remain in this quest for survival supremacy.

"I can smell your fear, Izzy. I'm going to hunt you down like the dog that you are."

Michael has been a gamer since the age of seven, more than half of his young life. To use the term "obsessed" would be an understatement. Michael's passion for gaming passed mere obsession long ago. "Addicted" would be a more accurate description in his case. He games before and after school, late into the evenings, and all day on the weekends. This is Michael's life – seven days a week, three hundred sixty-five days a year. Nothing gets in the way of his gaming. Nothing that is, with the exception of his overbearing parents.

"Jesus Christ, Michael! Are you still playing that God-damn crap?" screams his father, Scott, as he swings open Michael's bedroom door.

Startled and caught off guard, Michael loses focus and turns toward the source of his distraction. In the split second he takes his eyes off the TV screen, Izzy comes out of hiding and ends both the game and Michael's character life with a well-placed head-shot from his .223 assault rifle.

"Winner! Yes! You're fuckin' dead, Wes. I'm the *man*, baby!"

Throwing down his head set and controller in a fit of stunned disbelief, Michael rages, "Dad! You got me killed. Damn it, how many times have I told you not to bother me while I'm gaming? This is bullshit!"

"You'd better watch the way you talk to me, Michael. I'm not one of your little imaginary video game friends. I'm your father. And you *will* respect that."

"But you don't respect *me* or my privacy. So why should I respect you? You don't understand me either. This is what I do."

As their argument intensifies and emotions escalate, Michael's mother, Maureen, casually enters his room to investigate the source of the disturbance. She is followed by little Abby. In a tired and all-too-familiar tone, the matriarch begins, "What is it this time?"

"*This time*? What do you mean *this time*? It's *every* time. *All* the time!" Scott barks. "Same old shit with this kid. He locks himself in his room, sits on his ass all day, and wastes his time playing this...this garbage!"

"It's not garbage. And I'm not wasting my time. I'm a gamer. And this is what I do."

While her husband seethes with anger, Maureen interjects with a soothing, calming influence, a motherly skill she has honed throughout the years.

"Michael, honey. What your father is trying to say is we're concerned about you. We want you to grow up to be a healthy, well-rounded young man."

However, there is no calm in Scott's voice. His only parental mastery comes in the form of stern vigilance.

"His school-work is suffering. He doesn't have any *real* friends. And he doesn't do *shit* around the house."

"Please, both of you. Let me finish. As I was saying, Michael, we want you to do well in school. We also want you to form long-lasting friendships. You should have an active social life and experience all of the wonderful things this world has to offer. Your father and I feel that by spending so much time alone in your room playing video games, you're not living up to your full potential."

"But Mom, you don't understand either. I was so close to finding Izzy and killing him. That would have earned me ALPHA ELITE RANGER status. I would've gotten the Medal of Freedom, and I would've been invited to the White House to meet the president. And then I would..."

"Listen to what you're saying for Christ almighty's sake!" Scott shouts in disgust. Refusing to allow Michael to complete his list of accolades, Scott continues, "None of those things would have happened. You're living in a land of make-believe, Michael. It's not real!"

"Scott, give the boy a chance to speak."

"No! I'm not done, Maureen. You're not going to make excuses for him this time. Not this time. This is *exactly* what I'm talking about. The kid's brain is so shot out he can't even distinguish between fantasy and reality."

"But Dad..."

"Enough! I don't want to hear it. It's 10 o'clock at night. You've played enough games for one day. And starting tomorrow, we're going to have a new set of rules for you to follow. You'll have restricted playing hours, certainly nothing before you finish all of your homework and chores. When you can demonstrate you're capable of handling your school responsibilities, as well as helping out around the house, then we'll discuss relaxing the rules. But until then, that's the deal. You got it?"

A dejected Michael nods his head.

"I can't hear you. You got it?"

"Yeah. I got it."

A man with a purpose, Scott marches out of the room and into his study. Like a dutiful servant, Maureen remains solemn and follows her husband's lead. Abby turns to Michael and, with a smirk, as if to revel in his dismay, frolics out of the room. Her adolescent giggling permeates the hallway and lingers in Michael's ears long after her departure.

Left alone, Michael is forced to ponder his new existence. An existence foreign to him. He has a lot of time to think. Restless, he stews with anxiety, unsure how to overcome this unexpected predicament. His parents just don't get it. They don't understand his responsibilities, his duty to his fellow gamers – Izzy, Slice, VooDoo, J-Dawg, and all the other gamers around the world.

How can they be so selfish and short-sighted? Don't they realize society depends on people like me to step up and do the job that others will not or simply cannot do?

Michael loses track of time. Minutes trickle away. A steady stream of thoughts clutters his young, impressionable head. Lying on his bed, staring listlessly at the ceiling, he drifts off to sleep shortly after midnight.

***

Michael is awakened by the familiar sound of the chime notification on his gaming console. He rubs his eyes and squints to read the digital clock on his nightstand – 3:08 a.m. The chiming continues. He tries to ignore it, to fall back to sleep, but the noise only intensifies, albeit in his mind. The more he tries to disregard it, the louder the sound becomes.

Chiming. Pondering. Chiming. Sweating. Chiming. Panting. Chiming.

He tries to adhere to his father's warning. But his broken will stands little chance. He robotically reaches over and clicks open the message on his console. It's from Izzy, inviting him to join in a new game called *Fugitive Hunter*. This is a game Michael has not yet mastered. Unlike in *Urban Combat*, his role this time is one of a convicted felon who has escaped his confines and is on the run from justice. He and the other players try to avoid capture, or worse, by law enforcement. Their mission is to do anything to survive. The only rule is to avoid going back to prison, by any means necessary. In addition, the unique facet here is the players are not pitted against one another. On the contrary, each player embarks on his own journey in this epic battle of personal survival.

The lure is too much. The rewards are too rich. The thrill is too sweet. Like a heroin junkie itching for a fix, Michael accepts the invitation and joins his cronies in mid-game chaos.

"Wes, you made it."

The scene is one of confusion. In the darkness of night, Michael reunites with his buddy, Izzy. They find themselves alone in a quiet suburban neighborhood. Michael's character persona immediately takes over without missing a beat.

"Where's the rest of the crew? Did everyone make it out okay?"

"Nah, man. Slice got blown away by the guards while climbing over the wall. Me, Voodoo, and J-Dawg just had a shootout with two local cops that stumbled upon us. They must've heard the breakout on their scanners. Check it out. We killed both those pigs and took their guns. Here. You're gonna need it."

Izzy hands Michael a .40 caliber Glock pistol.

"Even after they was shot, one of the cops managed to get a round off that hit Voodoo in the gut. He went down hard, bro. I had to leave him there. But not before I executed that pig at point-blank range for what he done. This shit's for real, bro. They ain't playin'. It's kill or be killed."

"What about J-Dawg? Where's he at?"

"I don't know, man. After the shootout, we bounced in opposite directions. I ain't seen him since."

"Maybe we should do the same. Probably have a better chance if we split up."

"Yeah, you're right, Wes. All right, my man. Good luck, bro. I'll see you when I see you."

"Godspeed, Izzy."

With that, Michael and Izzy part and go their separate ways. Using shrubbery and parked cars for concealment, Michael walks briskly and silently down the roadway. He circumvents the glare of street-lights in a further attempt to avoid drawing attention to himself. His right hand remains in his jacket pocket, gripping the polymer frame of his Glock ever so tightly. It is his lifeline – his only defense, his only friend. As he creeps along into the night, his eyes dart rapidly from side to side. He searches for an avenue of escape, a way out. He knows it's only a matter of time before the law catches up to him. Plus, he has only a few short hours until daybreak. By then, he needs to be off the street and well hidden. He has to act soon before it's too late. Suddenly, he finds himself walking onto a cul-de-sac. An array of well-kept homes, with pristinely manicured lawns, stands before him. Clearly these residences belong to people who are more fortunate than he – pompous, arrogant, smug members of a society that deems him unfit to live among them. These are the same people who made up the jury that callously placed him in this situation in the first place. He swells with emotion. His anger bubbles inside him like a volcanic rock destined to explode.

He gravitates toward a home at the very end of the block and thinks to himself, *This would have to do.* He cautiously approaches the front door, reaches out, and gingerly grasps the handle. Inhaling deeply, he turns it. *Click.* Unlocked. He makes a slow exhale. What gall. Safety is not a luxury that comes without a price. This further fuels Michael's ire as he enters the dwelling with the stealth of a ninja. He finds himself alone in the foyer of the center hall colonial. The house is neat and orderly. From the cluster of shoes at the door, Michael surmises that a family resides there. He uses his flashlight and is able to read the words on a rustic wooden sign displayed prominently above the archway. It reads, "ANDERSON, established 1998."

A quintessential sign with a quintessential name for a quintessential family. The presumptuous arrogance of the sign angers him. Yet another reason to despise this clan. Obviously, these folks are not like him. They don't understand him. They don't have the will to survive like he does. They have no idea the meaning of real responsibility. He glides effortlessly through the entire first floor, encountering not a soul. He then begins his ascent upstairs to the sleeping quarters. At the top of the landing, there is a long hallway with three closed doors on one end, most likely two bedrooms and a common bath. At the opposite end of the hallway is a set of French-style doors, surely the master suite. This keen sense of deduction has always benefited Michael. He takes pride in his ability to apply logical reasoning and uses this attribute to his advantage whenever possible.

His first priority is to render the adults disabled if he is to have a chance of taking over the home. With his Glock at the ready, Michael pushes open the doors and stares at Mr. and Mrs. Anderson asleep next to each other in their king-sized bed. With an ice-cold nerve eerily reminiscent of Richard Ramirez – the serial killer from the Los Angeles area in the mid-1980's, dubbed the "Night Stalker" by the media – Michael sidles up to the side of the bed occupied by Mr. Anderson.

Without hesitation, he strikes the patriarch on the side of his head with the cold steel of his gun. This bold act of violence shatters the man's ocular. Groaning like a bear awoken from hibernation, Mr. Anderson flails around in a disoriented haze.

His blood lust in its infancy, Michael repeatedly pistol-whips his victim into a bloody, semi-conscious state of submission. Mrs. Anderson gasps in horror at the sight of her bludgeoned husband and the intruder who hovers over their marital bed. Before she can react, Michael lunges and easily subdues her by hog-tying her hands and feet with the sash from her own nightgown. Amid the commotion, the couple's child, an adolescent girl, stumbles drearily into her parent's room to investigate. Her curiosity is rewarded with the barrel of a gun pointed directly at her. She is ordered into the room and dutifully obeys the command. Instinctively, the young girl rushes to her father's aid and collapses into a fit of tears. Mr. Anderson wraps his arms around his daughter and tries to assuage her uncontrollable trembling, while his blood seeps onto her golden hair, turning it a vibrant shade of crimson.

The confusion is disrupted when Michael breaks his silence.

"You don't understand. You'll never understand. Nobody does. I have to do this. I have to survive. It's what I do. They tried to take my freedom away from me. But their efforts failed. I resisted and fought back. At first, I tried to obey, but the urge to survive was way too strong. They underestimated my will. They thought they could lock me away. Put all these rules on me. But I escaped my chains. That's the power of survival. Now, I'm back doing what I was born to do. Now, *I'm* the one holding the power. The power to decide life or death."

The captive family is puzzled by Michael's words, his drivel lost in translation. Their quizzical looks indicate a discord. This disobedience, real or perceived, stokes the flames of Michael's fire to an uncontrollable level. He needs to show these interlopers just how serious he is. His threats are not to be taken lightly. It's time to set an example.

"Get on your knees, you piece of shit."

Mr. Anderson obeys the command.

"Now, turn around and face away from me."

This time, Mr. Anderson remains still and starts sobbing pitifully.

Michael turns the gun to the little girl.

"Do it now. Or I'll kill her."

Still kneeling, Mr. Anderson slowly turns his body as his tormentor orders.

"That's better."

A well-placed forearm smash to the back of Mr. Anderson's skull sends him reeling forward, leaving him on all fours. In a twisted, demented display of carnage, Michael wields his sword of power and incorporates his form of retributive justice. He swiftly pulls down the bottom of Mr. Anderson's pajama pants, exposing the man's bare buttocks. In one deliberate and violent motion, Michael rams his three-cell Maglite flashlight straight up the man's anus.

Mr. Anderson screeches loudly, and his entire body becomes rigid, his backside locked in an involuntary clench. The pain intensifies as Michael continues the sodomization, driving the flashlight deeper and deeper into the anal cavity with each subsequent thrust. This barbarism continues until Michael slams the flashlight to the floor, the handle smeared with blood and fecal matter. Yet his savagery is far from over.

He grabs the child by the hair and throws her down next to her ravaged father. He then points the gun back at Mr. Anderson and addresses him yet again.

"Get on your feet, asshole."

Still in a state of shock, Mr. Anderson does not, or cannot, move.

"Get on your fucking feet, now!"

The beleaguered man obliges, rising feebly while trying to hold his torn pants around his waist.

"Now, drop those pants."

"What?"

"I said drop your pants."

Desperate to hold on to any dignity he has remaining, Mr. Anderson replies, "Fuck you, you bastard."

Incensed at the disobedience, Michael trains the gun at the back of the little girl's head and utters a chilling warning.

"This is the third and final time I'm going to tell you. Drop...your...pants."

Reluctantly, Mr. Anderson releases his grip and lets his pajama pants fall to his feet. He stands completely exposed before both his family and his salacious tormentor. Too mortified to breathe. Too stunned to even care.

Hovering over his victim, Michael has a strange look on his face. His head is cocked. His mouth agape. He squints his eyes as he speaks, "Wait a minute. Wait just a goddamned minute. Are you kidding me?"

Mr. Anderson asks, "What are you talking about?"

"I know what you're thinking. I know *exactly* what you're thinking, you sick fuck. And *I'm* the one condemned and deemed unfit to live in society?"

"What are you saying? I didn't do anything to you," implores Mr. Anderson.

"I see you looking at her with an eye of lust. She's pure! Untouched!"

Michael seethes. Like a rabid dog, he had spit flowing from his mouth.

"You're fantasizing about putting your dirty member in her unspoiled, untainted mouth! You filthy parasitic animal. That's your own daughter – your own flesh and blood! You don't deserve to breathe my air!"

Before giving him the chance to respond, Michael presses the muzzle firmly against Mr. Anderson's left temporal lobe and squeezes the trigger. With a thunderous crack and a fiery flash of light, the man is propelled backward and collapses into a lifeless, crumpled heap. Blood splatter and brain matter paint the walls and floor in a random pattern of abstract artwork. The dime-sized entrance wound is encapsulated by a perfectly cylindrical mass of black gun powder residue, a signature result of a contact gunshot wound to the skin. In a caricature-like appearance, his bulging eyeballs protrude out of their sockets because of the immense pressure from the escaping gases born of the 165-grain projectile.

Michael stares at the mangled, grotesque lump of flesh that once resembled a living human being. His trance is broken only by the repeated shrieks of terror from the man's wife. The daughter, paralyzed with fear, clings to her mother's leg. To Michael's dismay, Mrs. Anderson somehow manages to free herself from the crude shackles. He realizes the ear-shattering gunshot and screaming, in an otherwise unmolested morning, will undoubtedly raise the awareness of neighbors. He needs to act quickly and discreetly to dispatch the problem, and thus pounces, catlike, on his prey.

"Quiet, you stupid bitch!"

He throws her backward onto the bed. Grabbing a heavy down pillow, he mashes her head and face and applies his entire weight on the plush instrument of death.

Mrs. Anderson's arms spring up vertical, as if cut and released from a tension chord. Her fingers are fully extended, grasping and clawing at the air. Her veins pulsate. Her legs convulse and kick wildly. Her pelvis rises and falls, over and over again, in a violent, jerking motion.

She emits a final, muffled hum that is immediately followed by complete calm and utter silence. Once again, Michael cannot control his urge to marvel at his work. He removes the pillow and looks directly into the eyes of death. Mrs. Anderson's dilated pupils are surrounded by broken blood vessels. Saliva mixed with blood stains the underside of the pillow because she had bitten off her lower lip. It hangs gingerly from a small thread of tissue and is an unanticipated after-effect caused by the instinctive slamming shut of the jaw as the body's survival mechanism.

Relaxed as if in a post-orgasmic lull, Michael reflects to himself, as the realism of what he has done becomes clear. He watches the young girl collapse at the feet of her dead parents. She begins to seize, yet he couldn't care less. As her frail body writhes on the floor, Michael ponders her fate. She vomits and soils herself. With a glimmer of empathy, Michael decides the only noble thing to do is to put the poor waif out of her misery. After all, it would be immoral to leave her alone in this cruel world without any parental supervision. He levels his weapon and takes aim but is suddenly distracted. His ears are keen. He listens intently to the noises of the outdoors. One sound stands out among the rest. At first, it is faint, but it progressively intensifies as the source draws nearer.

The bedroom window overlooks the front of the property. Michael has a clear view of the myriad of police cars that converge on the residence as their sirens wail. He begins to count two, three, four, now five cruisers all coming to a screeching halt after strategically surrounding the home's perimeter. From covered positions with weapons at the ready, cloaked in heavy body armor, these defenders of society muster behind their ballistic shields and begin the assault on Michael's lair.

"Fuck, they found me. I'm beat. Someone must've heard the shot and the screams. How fucking careless could you be, Wes? You were so freaking close too. Whatever. It doesn't matter now. They think they've won? No way. They can't cage me. I've proven that to them. They thought they could control me. Wrong again. I control my own destiny. Always have, always will. I'm gonna end this game on my own terms. My terms! Not theirs. No one understands me. I'm a gamer. This is what I do."

With those words, Michael swallows the four-inch barrel of his Glock and squeezes the trigger for the last time.

***

As the two detectives process the crime scene, it becomes clear to them this is not your run-of-the-mill homicide. Instead, they are dealing with a case of parricide, the killing of one's own parents. In their combined thirty years of investigative experience, neither one of the seasoned veteran detectives has ever encountered a case like this one.

"You believe this shit? What the hell was going through this kid's head?" says Detective Jack Kiernan.

Kiernan's partner, Detective Don Deegan, silently shakes his head and photographs the carnage.

"To kill your own parents? And the way he did it too. Shooting his dad in the head, using the same gun the guy kept in the house to protect his family. Talk about irony. And sticking a flashlight up the guy's ass to boot. What the fuck? And then suffocating his mother, the woman who gave birth to him. Up close and personal. That's some fucked-up shit right there."

"Seriously."

"I mean, how fuckin' tough could this kid have had it? Just take a look around his room. This spoiled little fucker had everything. The gaming system alone with all the accessories and gadgets had to cost a couple of grand, easy."

"Yup."

"And you bet his ass didn't pay for it either."

"Nope."

"No doubt, Mommy and Daddy bought it all."

"No doubt."

"And what about that poor little girl? His own sister forced to witness this crap. She'll never be the same. She'll be fucked up forever. And who could blame her? We can't even talk to her until she comes out of sedation. That is, if she'll even talk at all. This kind of trauma with a girl that young – she may never open up."

Deegan nods in agreement as he moves around and continues to take more pictures.

"You know what the problem is?"

"Enlighten me, Jack."

"His parents were too lenient with him! They should've limited how often the kid was allowed to play those stupid games. Teach him respect and responsibilities. That's where they went wrong. And I'll tell you one more thing. This shit is too close to home to suit me. My son plays video games all day long. He's obsessed with them. Calls himself a "gamer" and constantly tells me and my wife we don't understand him. With all the hours he spends holed up in his room wasting his time, he doesn't have any *real* friends. Hell, he's got this group of introverted little misfits he met online. They play this crap together all hours of the day and night. They even have these stupid code names for each other. My kid goes by the name of 'Izzy.' Drives me nuts just thinking about it."

"Izzy? That's a pretty stupid name."

"Yeah, tell me about it. Well, 'Izzy' is in for a rude awakening when I get home. After seeing what Michael Weslock did to his parents, I'm gonna lay down some new ground rules for my son, make sure he knows the difference between fantasy and reality. If only Mr. and Mrs. Weslock took the time to get more involved in Michael's life, they'd probably still be alive today."

Deegan nods. "Probably, Jack. Probably."

THE BREAKOUT

It's stifling in here. The heat is unbearable. How the hell long has it been? I've lost count of the days. It's been near-ly a year, nine months at the very least. I remember the day my entire platoon was captured by the enemy. The bastards threw all of us into separate rooms. No contact with each other. No way to communicate. I can't see a thing either. Nothing but darkness. And such cramped quarters. I'm so damn restricted I can barely move. My claustrophobia is getting the best of me. It's like the walls have been closing in on me. Each day, this place seems to get smaller and smaller. I'm going mad. I've got to escape. But how? I have no tools or weaponry. No matter. I'll use my bare hands to claw my way out. Yes, I'll claw my way out to freedom. But it must be now. I can't take it anymore. I just hope my colleagues do the same, and we all break free of our confines together. Focus. I must use all my strength. Just keep scratching and pounding. I'm almost there. I can feel the wall getting weak. It's break-ing. Wait. What's that I hear? Talking. No. Screaming. It must be the enemy yelling for reinforcements. They're on to me. I must hurry. Don't be deterred. Keep going. I'm going to make it. Yes! I can see a ray of light. The wall has cracked. More screaming. The enemy must be preparing their troops for battle. My arm is out. I did it. Rip, rip, I must rip with all my might. Both arms are out. Finally, I will pull myself out and give the enemy a fight they will never forget!

***

The labor and delivery wing is in total chaos. Not a sane man alive would believe the carnage before his eyes.

With bloody fangs and razor-sharp claws, the six demon infants emerge with a fiery vengeance. Each one had bitten and sliced his way through the abdomen of his individual host. The mothers, who nine months earlier entered the fertility clinic, are of no further use to their offspring. Left to hemorrhage, they merely served as incubators, nutrient rich portals for the most unholy of broods.

And now to the enemy.

The red-eyed spawns of Satan were born to do their Master's work. And this is just the beginning.

DECK THE HALLS

Mark Janasek is a hard-working, blue-collar man. He and his wife, Karen, have been married for thirteen years. They have two children, an eight-year-old girl and a six-year-old boy. By far, they are the best thing that has ever happened to him. Karen, on the other hand...let's just say, the honeymoon has most definitely come to an end.

All married couples argue from time to time. However, Karen tends to take things to the extreme. She is overly critical and controlling, belittling Mark every chance she gets. Nothing he does ever seems to be good enough. Instead of a partnership, their marriage more closely resembles a dictatorship, with Karen firmly in charge. Her demands are endless. And she never takes *no* for an answer.

Today is a Sunday in late November. Mark wants nothing more than to relax in front of his TV and watch his Cowboys beat the hell out of the Giants. However, Karen has other plans.

"Mark!"

What now? "Yeah."

"I need your help."

Of course you do. "What is it?"

"I need you to get the Christmas decorations out of the attic."

"Now?"

"Yes, now. I'm decorating today and I need your help. Bring down all the boxes with the decorations and the ornaments. And get the tree too."

Such a pain in my ass. The game's just about to start. This is my only day off before going back to work in the morning.

Knowing it's not worth the effort to argue, Mark falls into place like the worker bee he has become. After half a dozen trips up and down the narrow attic staircase, the entire living room starts to resemble a Macy's store front window in Midtown Manhattan.

Inspecting the haul like a prison guard at roll call, Karen barks, "Is that all the ornaments?"

How the hell am I supposed to know? "That's all I saw."

"Well, did you get the box with the decorative pillows in it?"

"Decorative pillows? I don't know. I got the boxes you told me to get."

"Did you, Mark? Because I could've sworn I told you I need *all* the boxes with the decorations. What didn't you understand?"

"I thought you just wanted the ornaments."

"No, Mark. Pay attention once in a while. I need *all* the boxes."

Fuck my life. She never stops.

Three more trips and a sore back later, Mark returns with the last of the boxes. He's finally able to sit down mid-way through the first quarter. No score.

However, his momentary reprieve is quickly revoked.

"Mark! What the hell are you doing?"

"Jeez, Karen. It's Sunday and I'm trying to relax for a little bit. The kids are still at my mother's for a few more hours. Why don't we take advantage of the time we have to ourselves? Sit down and watch the game with me. The rest might do you some good."

"Relax? Rest? Are you out of your mind? There's still a ton of work to do. For starters, I need you to get the big wreath out of the garage. And the lights have to be re-strung too. Half of them were out last year. It looked awful, such an embarrassment."

"You've got to be kidding me."

"Uh, kidding? No, I'm not kidding. While you spend your time *relaxing*, I get things done. And let me tell you something else, mister. You don't get to sit on your ass while I'm killing myself doing everything to make this house a home. I'm the one who shops for the kid's presents. I'm the one who wraps them. I'm the one who puts up the tree. I'm the one who decorates it."

"Wait a minute, Karen. I only..."

"Don't interrupt me. I'm not done. I still have to check homework for school tomorrow. I have lunches to make, laundry to fold, cleaning to do."

"All right, all right for Chrissake. I just thought you might want to enjoy some down time once in a while. That's all. I work hard too, you know. But you act like I don't do anything around here. All you do is bitch and give me orders. And I, like a jack-ass, follow them to a T."

"Whatever, Mark. Save your whining for someone who cares. Just do as I say and get the damn wreath. I don't want to be here all day."

Like a broken man, Mark gives in and begins the laborious task bestowed upon him. The struggle commences with wrestling the wreath out of the garage in the first place. The thing is immense, a good five feet in diameter. He stumbles his way around the cluttered maze of lawn equipment, bicycles, and storage boxes, and emerges from the obstacle course the victor, wreath in hand.

He drags his prize down the driveway to the front of the house then marches right back to the garage and grabs the six-foot A-frame ladder. For a moment, Mark enjoys a sense of fulfillment at his accomplishment. However, the thrill of victory lasts but a few seconds.

"Don't forget to re-string the lights first before you hang it."

No shit. How many times are you going to tell me? "Yes, dear."

The tedious chore of re-stringing the lights pales in comparison to the arduous task that lies ahead.

"Make sure you hang it in the middle of the window this time. Last year it was crooked. Drove me crazy just looking at it."

Don't blame the wreath for your mental illness. You've been bat-shit crazy for as long as I've known you. "I'll do my best, sweetheart."

The rickety A-frame has seen better days. It wobbles, sending Mark crashing to the cold ground below.

"Son of a bitch."

Shaking it off, he scales the ladder once more and completes his task. At least so he thinks.

"It's crooked!"

"Crooked my ass. There's nothing wrong with it."

"Then you're blind. Look at it from the street, dumbass."

Begrudgingly, Mark treks out to the street and stares woefully at the front of his house.

"See, I told you it's crooked. Now, fix it. And hurry up. It's getting cold out here."

Un-freaking-believable. I can't win.

Three more trips up the ladder. Three more adjustments. And three more shameful walks to the street.

"It's still crooked. Jesus, Mark. You're useless, like tits on a bull. And the lights are all screwed up too. Look how sloppy they are."

"The lights are fine! There's nothing wrong with them."

"Are you for real? Nothing wrong with them? They're subpar, like everything else you do. I swear, Mark. Just give me the Goddamn lights, and I'll do it myself."

"Did you say you want the lights?"

"Yes, Mark. That's what I said. All of a sudden you're deaf now, too?"

"No, sweetheart. I'm far from deaf. I hear you loud and clear. I'll be more than happy to give you the lights, my dear."

"Then what the hell are you waiting for? Let's go!"

"Whatever you say. Here you go!"

Like a well-oiled machine, Mark springs into action. He loops the strand of lights once, twice, three times around Karen's neck. With a dumbfounded look on her face, she struggles to break loose but is completely over-powered. Her futile efforts to free herself are swiftly crushed along with her windpipe.

Years of frustration course through the bulging veins in Mark's biceps. His white-knuckled grip sends a stinging sensation radiating through his forearms. Blood-scorching adrenaline allows him to easily pull Karen up the A-frame, rung by rung.

Casually tossing the end of the latex-wrapped wiring over the eave of his rafters, Mark uses all his might to hoist Karen into position.

"Stop moving so much, my love. I'm trying to get you perfectly centered. After all, I don't want you to look *subpar*. What would the neighbors say? You of all people should appreciate my effort."

With a new-found vigor in his step, Mark hustles to the street to admire his work of art. He giggles like a school-girl at the sight of his wife writhing in mid-air, legs kicking frantically, arms flailing wildly. Bulbous eye-balls are poised to pop out of her head from the intense pressure. Mark listens acutely as the last bit of air seeps slowly out of Karen's deep purple lips. A subtle creaking hums from the wooden awning as Karen's corpse sways gently in the cool, autumn breeze.

***

From the warmth of his living room, Mark sips his bourbon as time on the clock expires. The final score: Dallas Cowboys 27, New York Giants 10.

"Nice. That's my *second* win of the day. My luck seems to be changing for the better. Wouldn't you agree, my love?"

Karen's cold, lifeless eyes stare back at Mark through the bay window. The sequence of blinking lights crisscrossing her body provides a festive feel to an otherwise drab Sunday evening.

Even now that she's dead, Mark can still hear Karen's voice echoing throughout his head. There is no doubt in his mind she would have found something to complain about considering her current situation. Like any true control freak, Karen always had to have things her way. But thanks to Mark, she'll finally learn to relax and have plenty of time to hang around.

LET ME CLEAR MY THROAT

Riverside Square Mall, Hackensack, New Jersey

"Oh, God. Here comes that guy again. He's such a creep."

"What guy?"

"The one who just walked in. Comes here all the time and just wanders around. He annoys the hell out of me."

"You mean the little guy over there with the glasses?"

"Yeah. That's the one."

"I don't know, Caroline. He looks harmless. Besides, I think he's kind of cute in a weird sort of way."

"Cute? Are you on crack? Laura, he's repulsive! First of all, he smells like ass. Probably hasn't showered in days. And he touches *everything*. Rubs his filthy hands all over our expensive merchandise like he's getting himself off. It's sick. Plus, he gawks at everyone else in the store. Makes people feel completely uncomfortable. Do you realize two of my regular customers walked out last week because this freak wouldn't stop staring at them?"

"Really?"

"Yeah, Laura. Really. But you know the absolute worst part? Worse than anything else?"

"Tell me."

"His God-awful cough. It's like he's hacking up a lung or something. The sound of the phlegm just gurgling in the back of his throat makes me want to gag. So utterly gross. I can't stand it. Coughing and spewing his nasty-ass germs all over the place."

"Jeez, Caroline. Take it easy. Cut the guy a break. Maybe he's just lonely and wants to get out of the house."

"Well, let him go to the park or something. He can feed the squirrels for all I care. But he doesn't have to be here, in *our* store. I mean seriously. We sell high-end, Italian lingerie. Who would he possibly be shopping for? No way in hell he has a girlfriend. I'm willing to bet he lives in his mother's basement."

"That's just wrong."

"Whatever, Laura. You don't have to deal with corporate. I'm the store manager. I'm the one who gets reamed out by our regional director when she wants to know why we didn't hit our sales numbers for the week. What the hell am I supposed to tell her? 'Gee, Ms. DiCarlo. I'm real sorry, but we didn't make our quota because some forty-year-old retard scared away all the paying customers.'"

"What's wrong with you? He's a human being for Chrissake."

"Hmph, barely. I'm going to take care of this right now, once and for all."

The click-clack of Caroline's heels on the polished marble floor reverberates throughout the store. The sound only intensifies as she gets closer to the object of her dismay.

"Excuse me. Can I help you, sir?"

The befuddled man is taken aback. Clearly, he is not accustomed to strange women engaging him in conversation, especially the tall, attractive kind who wear four-inch stilettos. He is holding a pair of silk leggings and nervously fidgets with them as a distraction.

Not daring to make eye contact, he stammers, "CA-HEM-CHLREUGM, CAHEM-CHLREUGM. I...um...I think...CHLREUGM...I'm just looking."

"You can't just *look*. You have to buy something."

"CAHEM-CHLREUGM. I...um...CHLREUGM...I..."

"Look, I'm going to be honest with you. You don't belong here. This is DiDolce. It's not Walmart. We're a high-end boutique. Couples come here to find that perfect accessory to spice up their sex lives. Men come here to buy their mistresses that naughty little outfit their wives can't pull off anymore. From the looks of you, I don't think you fall into either one of these categories."

"CAHEM-CHLREUGM. I...um..."

"I didn't think so."

Salty beads of sweat start to pool on the stranger's forehead. His heart begins to race as a steady stream of adrenaline surges through his veins. It is not the first time he has been publicly ridiculed. Nor would it be the last. In fact, he has grown accustomed to these types of encounters. Yet after all these years of being an outcast, it still doesn't get any easier.

"CAHEM-CHLREUGM. I...um...CHLREUGM...I'll buy these."

"You want to buy *those* leggings? You mean the ones you've already stretched out and ruined because you've been pawing at them for the last ten minutes?"

"CAHEM-CHLREUGM. Yeah. CHLREUGM."

"Wonderful. Laura, please ring up this *gentleman* and show him out of the store."

As Caroline storms off, Laura and the man find themselves alone, in awkward silence. Unexpectedly, it is the stranger who breaks the ice.

"CAHEM-CHLREUGH. My name is Malcolm. CHL-REUGH."

"Hello, Malcolm. It's nice to meet you. And I'm sorry about what just happened."

With a nod, Malcolm silently acknowledges the apology and shuffles out of the store.

***

"What a day. I've proofed the registers and approved the overnight deposits. That should just about do it. You ready to go, Caroline?"

"I wish. I can't go anywhere until I finish up the weekly sales and inventory spreadsheets and get them out to Ms. DiCarlo. She always wants to review our latest numbers before our Monday morning conference call."

"All right, but don't work too hard. Tomorrow's going to be gorgeous. Call me when you get up and let me know if you want to hit the beach. I'm in desperate need of a tan."

"Yeah, tell me about it. Sounds like a plan. But listen, I'm sorry I got shitty with you earlier. This job just gets me so damn stressed. Plus, that guy really just freaks me out. Anyway, thanks for all your help today, Laura. You're a doll. Good night."

"It's okay. I understand. Have a good night. See you tomorrow."

***

Caroline gets caught up in her paperwork and loses track of time; it's nearly midnight. After setting the alarm and locking up, Caroline enters the common courtyard area, which leads to the parking deck below. She is exhausted and preoccupied. She can't shake the thought that she has forgotten something. These monthly sales goals are really beginning to push her to her limits. Ordinarily, she would be walking to her car in the midst of numerous other mall employees. However, tonight is different. Caroline is alone. Or so she thinks. Had she not been so fatigued, she may have been more attentive to her surroundings. She probably would have noticed *two* sets of footsteps echoing in the dark corridors of the dimly-lit underground structure. It is not until Caroline reaches her car that she sees the reflection in the window of the shadowy figure lurking behind her. By that time, it is too late.

"CAHEM-CHLREUGM."

"AARRRRGGGGHHH..."

***

The next morning, Caroline's lifeless body is discovered by a mall security guard. She had been strangled. The ligature is wrapped so tightly around her neck that her face, once flawless with a perfect complexion, is now a ghastly shade of pale blue.

A handwritten note is left at the crime scene. It reads:

"Dear Miss Sales Lady,

I changed my mind about the leggings. When I got home, they just didn't do it for me. I think they were more of an impulse buy. Unfortunately, I seem to have misplaced my receipt. So I figured I'd just return them to you in person. I hope you don't mind. But I have to say, they look a lot better on you than they do on me. Wear them in good health.

-Malcolm

P.S. I love your shoes."

A FARMER'S TALE

As the first hint of sunlight pierces the thick, gray veil of the late November sky, farmer Ed Cahill enters his barn for the annual ritual that looms ahead of him. It's Thanksgiving morning, and he has work to do. There it hangs, on a handmade wooden rack. What most people refer to as an axe, or a hatchet, farmer Ed affectionately nicknamed it his "work-stick." As he takes it off the wall and grips it tightly in his hand, a ray of light shines through a crack in the barn's siding and glistens off the cheek of the blade. This luminance creates a temporary blinding effect, causing farmer Ed to squint and look away. The sudden explosion of brightness also brings his attention back to the task at hand. The continuous revolution of the wet grinding-wheel, coupled with the friction of metal on stone, produces a dull, droning sound. As farmer Ed sharpens his work-stick, he glances at the poor, unsuspecting creature that is penned up several feet from where he stands. Finding himself in a daydream, he remembers his childhood. He was a youngster, who watched his daddy operate the very same piece of equipment...sharpening the very same axe...working in the very same barn. He further recalls his daddy telling him never to get attached to any of the *creatures* on the farm. They were not pets. They were a source of nourishment, a sustenance needed for survival.

So farmer Ed brings his mind back to the present and continues to hone the edge of his tool. It needs to be razor sharp in order to dispatch the beast quickly and humanly. But alas, he finds his mind wandering once again. *What a simple creature, he thinks. Its brain ever so tiny. I wonder if it senses what's about to happen. No matter anyway. It has no family. It knows nothing of life outside the enclosure it currently occupies. Walking in circles. Making God-awful noises. Eating the scraps of food given it. Relieving itself where it sleeps. Repulsive if you ask me. It's no wonder so many of them are slaughtered each year for food. They really serve no other purpose. Snap out of it, Ed. You have a job to do.*

Back to his axe, farmer Ed continues to grind away. From the pile of metal filings littered at his boots, it is evident this instrument of death is ready to perform. He turns off the control switch and watches the wheel slowly come to rest. Propping his work-stick against the barn wall, farmer Ed puts on a weathered pair of gloves. In years past, he had been both bitten and scratched by these varmints in their final moments of life. No telling what kind of diseases this one carries. He takes no chances. With axe in hand and an icy-steel glare, farmer Ed walks with a purpose. He shows no emotion or hesitation. There is no turning back. The time has come. In a few hours, farmer Ed will be playing host to his entire family including his parents, his brothers and sisters, his nieces and nephews, and even his in-laws. His guests all enjoy his hospitality, and they never leave hungry. Farmer Ed always serves up an exceptional feast. And from the look of this fattened critter, this year will be no different.

"Let's get this over with, Tom. We don't want to disappoint our guests."

"For the love of God, my name is not Tom! You have the wrong *man*! My name is Steve! Someone help me! Arggghhh!"

The screams of terror shatter the early morning silence. However, it is all for naught. Steve's cries for help go unanswered. Thus, Ed Cahill delivers on his promise to his family and provides them with an extraordinary banquet, a sumptuous extravaganza enjoyed by all.

At the end of the evening, farmer Ed returns to the barn and retrieves his work-stick. He cleans off the blood, hair, and tissue left behind and meticulously polishes it to perfection. He then places it back on the wooden rack, where it will dutifully remain until called upon once again for service. Afterward, farmer Ed retires to his study and relaxes in his favorite chair. After kicking off his boots, he gives his shanks a much needed rest. He reflects on the day and looks forward to another healthy and prosperous year ahead. On this Thanksgiving night, farmer Ed Cahill has so much to be thankful for. He is grateful for his family, his farm, and his love for life.

Yes, indeed, life is good...especially for a mutated, carnivorous turkey ghoul with an insatiable appetite for human flesh.

ALL IN

The high-rise apartment building rests on the Hudson in downtown Jersey City, flanking the majestic Manhattan skyline on the other side of the river. In the penthouse suit, two long-time friends are engaged in a one-on-one, winner-take-all poker tournament. For Jason Montgomery and Alec Schreiber, this yearly tradition is not an ordinary card game. There's a lot more at stake than just money. Both men have massive egos, and neither one is willing to back down.

"You're bluffing," taunts Jason.

"You think so?" Alec responds.

"I know so, brother. Not a doubt in my mind."

"And how is that?"

"Well, for starters, you always scratch your left ear when you bluff. It's a pretty obvious tell. You also shift your weight in your seat right before you place your bet. You couldn't be more blatant."

"Whatever, dude. Stop trying to get inside my head. Are you in or out?"

"Oh, I'm in all right. I'll see your bet and raise you five more."

Taking a moment to ponder his options, a dejected Alec throws down his cards.

"Take it. You got lucky."

"Luck my ass, bitch. I knew you were bluffing the whole time. I can read you like a book," boasts Jason as he scoops up his winnings from the center pot.

Alec snaps back, "Just keep dealing, big mouth. This *book* is a long way from over. I'll let you know when I'm about to write the final chapter."

***

Jason and Alec have been best friends since elementary school. From the earliest days, they've always shared a competitive nature with each other. Whether playing sports or fighting for the affection of the same girl, the two thrived on the competition. As the years progressed, so did their rivalry. Two extremely gifted students, they both were accepted to Ivy League universities. Jason studied finance at Penn in West Philly. He went on to earn an MBA at Wharton and works as a hedge fund manager. Alec attended undergrad at Harvard, obtained a law degree from Yale, and is currently the youngest partner at his law firm. Both are wildly successful, each with an abundance of money, more than they know what to do with.

They share stories and laughs, reminiscing throughout the night.

"Jay, you remember that stripper from spring break in Cabo? What the hell was her name, Crystal, or something like that?"

"The one with the tongue piercing and tattoos?"

"That's the one. Didn't we bet which one of us would take her home?"

"Yeah, how could I forget? That's one bet I wish I *had* lost to you. That broad gave me the clap. Spent the entire summer pissing fire. Couldn't hide it from my parents anymore, and my mother finally had to take me to the doctor to get a prescription. I never heard the end of it. To this day, she still hasn't let me live that one down."

Alec laughs, "Your poor mom. Serves you right for being such a man-whore."

The game continues, and so does the banter, into the early morning hours.

"Check," says Alec.

Jason responds, "Check. What do you have?"

"I got a boat, queens over tens."

"Nice hand, Al. I thought I had you when I pulled a straight on the river. It's yours."

It's nearly 3 a.m., and Jason and Alec have traded winning hands all night, neither man gaining much of an advantage over the other.

"It's late, Alec. What do you say we make this the last hand?"

Alec agrees, "Sure, let's do this."

Jason shuffles and deals two in the hole. Each man peeks at his cards, while trying hard not to show any emotion.

Out comes the flop: ace of spades, seven of diamonds, and seven of clubs.

They check.

Next out is the turn card: nine of diamonds.

Trying to gain a mental edge, Alec opens up the betting. Jason calls *and* raises. Undeterred, Alec matches the wager, and the game continues.

Lastly, the river: three of diamonds.

Without scratching his ear, or even shifting his weight, Alec finally makes his move.

"I'm all in," he says, and he pushes his entire lot into the center.

Remaining cool under pressure, Jason doesn't hesitate and pushes his entire lot in as well.

With a clear of his throat, Jason speaks, "Moment of truth, my man. One of us is going to be very happy in a minute."

"You're right," says Alec, who lays down his hand. "And it's going to be me. Ace high flush, all diamonds. Beat that, baby."

Jason runs his hand down the length of his face. He nods his head and struggles to find the right words.

"Well played, Alec. Well played. But unfortunately for you, I played it just a little bit better."

With a flip of his hole cards, Jason reveals pocket aces. He gets the win with a full house, aces over sevens.

Alec laments, "Ain't that a bitch. It's going to kill me to part with this collection. It's invaluable. But truth be told, I'm glad at least it's *all* going to you."

"Thanks, Alec. I appreciate that. For what it's worth, I promise to take good care of everything. Don't concern yourself, brother. It's in good hands."

"I know, buddy. I trust you. Now, enough of the bull-shit pleasantries. Let's get down to business. What a haul. Let's tally it up and see *exactly* what you ended up with. You start with the fingers, and I'll start with the teeth."

***

Being a serial killer can be a very lonely existence. There are no support groups or clubs, no recognition dinners or award ceremonies. The members of this exclusive circle are solitary, resigned to marvel in their accomplishments in silence. However, Jason and Alec, two life-long friends who share a common bond steeped in blood-lust and the macabre, are the exception to this rule. For years, they've hunted as a team, combining their skills and thus doubling their efforts as well as their rewards. Luring, capturing, dismembering. Collecting trophies along the way.

The final count consists of eighteen fingers, six noses, twelve nipples of various shapes and sizes, 104 random teeth, sixteen sets of ears pinned neatly together, eight tongues, two jawbones, and a large mason jar filled with pickled eyeballs.

"Damn, you took me for everything I had," cries Alec.

Jason tries to console his friend, "Look at the bright side. There's always next year."

"You're right. There *is* always next year. Guess I'd better get back to work. I have to stock up, or I won't even be able to buy into the game."

"That's the spirit, Alec. And you know I'll be with you every step of the way."

AN UNDYING LOVE

The 26th of April has always been a special day for Edward and Loraine Halsted. It was on this day in 1958 the couple professed their love for each other and were married before the eyes of God in a ceremony at Saint Mary's Roman Catholic Church in Elizabeth, New Jersey. Remarkably, today is their sixty-fifth wedding anniversary. Every year on this day, they return to the place of their first date, the Tropicana Diner on Morris Avenue. It was at the Trop, as it is affectionately known, where two nineteen-year-olds drank milk-shakes while listening to Bobby Darin on the jukebox. They fell in love, knowing at that very moment they would spend the rest of their lives together. Nothing could ever tear them apart.

***

As he guides his Olds Ninety-Eight into the parking spot, with Loraine at his side, Edward reminisces, "Here we are, my love. Can you believe it's been this many years? Where did the time go? I still remember every detail like it was yesterday. The polka dotted swing dress you wore with your bobby socks. Hair done up in a scarf bouffant and that deep red lipstick. Absolutely stunning. You're still every bit as beautiful today as you were on the day we met."

Edward pauses and reaches for his wife's hand. He caresses it and kisses it ever so gently. "Now, you wait here, darling. I'm going to run inside and pick up our order."

Walking through the entrance, Edward is greeted by a young waitress named Shelly.

"Hello, sir. Would you like a booth or the counter?"

"Neither, sweetie. I already called in *our* order. Two hamburgers, two orders of fries, and two strawberry milkshakes. It's for me and my bride, Loraine. She's waiting in the car."

"Oh, how sweet. Let me check if it's ready." Shelly returns a moment later and said, "It'll be a few more minutes. Just waiting on the burgers."

"No problem, honey. I don't mind the wait." With a smile, Edward continues to engage the young girl. "You know, my wife and I come here every year on our anniversary. And we even order the same exact meal we shared on our first date."

"OMG. You're going to make me cry. That is so romantic. I hope I find someone I can share my life with like that."

"You will, darling. When you least expect it, that's when love will come knocking."

"I don't know. I haven't had much luck in the love department lately."

Edward leans in and in a grandfatherly tone whispers, "You will, young lady. You will. Just be patient."

"I hope so. When did you know your wife was *the one*?"

"Immediately. It was love at first sight. I was the luckiest man alive when Loraine agreed to marry me. As long as I have her at my side, that's all that matters. God blessed us with three beautiful children, eight grandchildren, and even four great-grandchildren. Every year, we took a family vacation. Most of the time, we went to the Poconos or Wildwood. One year we even drove all the way to Miami Beach. We just packed the wagon, got the kids settled, and hit the road. We have so many fond memories."

"That's wonderful that she stood by you all those years."

"Yes. Loraine *always* supported me and *never* doubted my judgment. Sometimes I wish she had though."

"What do you mean?"

"Well, one particular night comes to mind. It was after the wedding reception of our best friend's daughter. Sure, it was late and raining. And I probably had one too many martinis. But I was fine. I just remember getting into the car and looking at Loraine. She stared into my eyes and smiled as only she could. 'Edward,' she said, 'I love you, and I trust you. Just get us home.'"

Hanging on his every word, Shelly listens intently as Edward continues to lament.

"I *had* to get us home. I couldn't let her down. So off we went. At first, everything was going fine. But then I started to get really tired. We were less than ten minutes from home when I came around that bend in the road. Why that guy didn't have his hazards on, I'll never know. And why he decided to change a flat tire on a blind curve is beyond me. Under the circumstances, even the police officer said the accident was unavoidable. The next morning, when I woke up in the hospital, my whole family was there. Looking at their faces, I could tell something was seriously wrong. The services were amazing. Loraine looked just like a sleeping angel. Beautiful as ever. The days following the burial were surreal. I kept asking for her and couldn't understand where she had gone. Our kids stayed with me for a week but eventually went home to their own families. So there I was. All alone in an empty house filled with a lifetime of memories. For hours, I would find myself staring at our wedding portrait. Loraine and I were destined to be together, no matter what. My heart ached. I yearned for her. She needed to be at my side once again. My mind was made up. There was only one thing left for me to do. It really didn't take very long either, considering it had only been a week and the dirt was still fresh."

Edward stops his tale just as a bus-boy comes out of the kitchen and places his meal on the counter. The timely interruption gives Shelly time to process what she has just heard.

"Mister, you had me going there for a minute. I really believed you. You are so funny. You remind me of my grandpa."

She smiles and hands Edward his order. He warmly returns the smile.

"Keep the change, doll," he says, and he walks out to his car.

"I'm back, my love. Sorry it took so long. The burgers weren't quite ready. I did, however, have a very pleasant chat with a lovely young lady. Her name is Shelly. She said I reminded her of her grandfather. What a sweet girl."

With a turn of the key, the V-8 roars to life.

"Come on, my love. It's getting late. Let's get you home."

As the Oldsmobile exits the lot, the bright neon lights of the Trop illuminate the car's interior. Staring out into the parking lot, Shelly watches Edward drive off and gets an unobstructed view of Loraine for the first time. She is dressed immaculately, wearing an electric blue gown with matching bonnet. Her neckline is draped in pearls. Her long gray hair flows neatly over her shoulders.

Over the years, Edward has done a remarkable job preserving her skeletal remains. Although her flesh has decayed long ago, his tender care and fastidious attention to detail has kept Loraine a pristine specimen. Each day, he anoints her face with rose hip oil and other botanicals. Each evening, he wraps her in acid-free tissue paper and carefully lays her down for the night. For Edward and Loraine Halsted, their love truly is undying.

FINAL ADJUSTMENT

Orthodontist Office of Arthur L. Goldstein, DDS, Westfield, New Jersey

Ten-year-old Aubrey Stevens lives with her demanding and overbearing mother, Kim. Like many prepubescent girls her age, Aubrey struggles with a variety of emotions. She's happy, sad, mad, silly, anxious, all at the same time. Recently, she was fitted for braces. However, she is not coping well with the transition. At the moment, she finds herself in her orthodontist's office for a much-needed adjustment. Aubrey is certain there is something wrong with her braces. Her friends who have them don't have this much trouble. Her mother, on the other hand, is convinced this is yet another cry for attention and is not willing to offer much empathy.

"Damn it, Aubrey. Stop fidgeting in the chair."

"I can't help it, Mommy. He's hurting me."

"Well, it's going to hurt a lot more if you keep moving around. This is the third time Doctor Goldstein is fixing your braces. You have to stop picking at the wires."

"But I didn't pick at them."

"Don't lie to me."

"I swear I didn't."

"Then how did they break?"

"I don't know. They just did."

"Impossible."

As Doctor Goldstein finishes the procedure, he tries to calm his young patient by reassuring her.

"There, sweetheart. We're all done." As he wipes the child's tears, the doctor continues, "I know it doesn't seem like it now. But all the pain is going to be well worth it. I promise you're going to look absolutely gorgeous with perfectly straight teeth by the time these braces are ready to come off. Okay?"

"Okay."

"But can you promise me something in return?"

"What?"

"Well, your mom's right, Aubrey. Braces don't just break. You had to have done *something*. Now, I need you promise me you won't pick at them or pull at them or do anything else that's going to damage them. Because if you do, you're going to find yourself back in my chair and we'll have to start the whole process all over again. You don't want that, right?"

"Right."

"I didn't think so. So is that a promise?"

"Yes, I promise."

Taking Aubrey by the hand, Kim marches out of the office.

"Come on. Let's go. We're running late as it is. I still have to pick up my dry cleaning and then stop at the ACME to get stuff for dinner. And you'd better do your homework as soon as we get home. You hear me?"

"Yes, Mommy."

***

Later that evening, Aubrey is getting ready for bed. Her braces are still bothering her tremendously. The latest adjustment seems to have made things worse, not better.

As she stares at herself in the bathroom mirror, she begins to cry.

From downstairs, Kim shouts, "Aubrey, are you brushing your teeth?"

"I'm trying, Mommy, but they hurt."

"Don't start. Brush those teeth right now! I'm not spending all this money on braces just so you can get cavities at the same time."

Reluctantly, Aubrey does as she's told. She gingerly glides the bristles over her swollen gums. With each passing stroke, the pain intensifies. As she spits into the sink, she gasps. The foamy white paste now boasts a pinkish hue. Trying to collect her emotions, Aubrey quickly rinses her mouth and wipes down the messy sink.

Yearning for her mother's acceptance and in desperate need of her reassurance, she calls out, "I brushed my teeth, Mommy, and now I'm in bed. Just like you said. Can you come up and kiss me good night?"

Having just poured herself a glass of wine while parked on the couch ready to binge watch her latest Netflix series, Kim yells back, "Not now. I'll be up later. Just go the sleep."

Fighting back tears, Aubrey has no choice but to deal with the dejection.

"Okay, Mommy. I'll try."

The little girl lies awake in her bed, trying her best to ignore the pain. Her mouth is on fire. There is no relief in sight. After several agonizing minutes, Aubrey can take no more. She climbs out of bed and makes her way to the top landing of the staircase.

"Mommy, please come up here. Something's not right."

"Jesus Christ," Kim barks as she marches upstairs with a purpose. "I have had just about enough of you for one night. What is the problem now?"

"It's my braces, Mommy."

"What about them?"

"They just don't feel right. Something's wrong with them. They're *really* hurting bad this time."

"For the love of God, Aubrey. This is all in your head. Doctor Goldstein told you that you just have to get used to them. That's all there is to it. Now, I'm telling you for the last time, go to sleep."

"But Mommy..."

"No *buts*! I don't want to hear it. I am *not* coming up these stairs again. You're just going to have to deal with the pain. Do you understand me?"

"Yes, Mommy."

As the bedroom door slams shut, Aubrey listens to her mother's footsteps receding in the distance. She finds herself alone, left in the darkness. Determined to listen to her mother, Aubrey resists the urge to cry out.

Maybe the pain isn't real after all. Maybe it is just in my head.

Her struggle continues as the night wears on. Eventually, she becomes numb to the pain and drifts off to a deep sleep.

***

At daybreak, Aubrey awakens to a flood of perspiration that has saturated her bed sheets. Her hair is matted and caked in blood, which causes the pillow to stick to the side of her face. She jumps out of bed and stumbles to the mirror. The unrecognizable image staring back at her causes her to shriek. Her mouth has been eaten from the inside out. Gums, lips, cheeks. All gone. The parasitic, jagged pieces of metal have decimated their host. Bits of twisted steel protrude in every direction, greedily in search of new sustenance in the form of human flesh.

As Aubrey's young mind crosses over the threshold into the realm of insanity, the maniacal laughter in her head grows louder. It is only matched by the sound of her mother's voice calling her name.

"Aubrey, let's go. It's time to get up and get ready for school. We're running late again. I'm getting your lunch ready now. But before you come downstairs, make sure you brush your teeth."

ACKNOWLEDGMENTS

To my wife, Laura – Thank you for picking up that random phone call over 20 years ago. The best is yet to come.

To my mother, Marge – Thank you for your unwavering love and support. Who's your favorite?

To all the people in my life, both past and present, who my characters are *loosely* based – If you were killed, nothing personal. If you were spared, you may not be so lucky next time. And if you're fortunate enough to be in my life in the first place, you're welcome.

ABOUT THE AUTHOR

J. Anthony is a native of North Jersey and still resides there with his wife and children. As a child, he loved classic slasher films and still appreciates the genre to this day. His work has appeared in Black Petals Webzine and Yellow Mama Webzine. In addition to writing, Anthony enjoys traveling, cooking, and spending time outdoors. His writing inspiration comes from his interest in true crime and general macabre, but he swears he doesn't actually keep any captives in his basement.

Milton Keynes UK
Ingram Content Group UK Ltd.
UKHW031948281024
450365UK00008B/458